FESTIVE FLING

LEE WILLIAMSON

FIRST KISS PRESS

PART ONE
FESTIVE FLING

KAYLA

Rolling down the window, I allow the sea breeze to waft over my face, letting it cool me down and clear my head. Liam talks on in my ear and I force my attention back from the azure blue waves and the sparkling golden sand.

The scene outside is so tranquil it's hard to believe I'm on the Central Coast of New South Wales, only just over an hour and a half from the hustle and bustle of Sydney. The drive up to Nords Wharf was relaxing, but I'd had to pay more attention to my driving when I turned towards Middle Camp Beach. My little blue car struggled on the bumpy gravel road to the carpark at the beach's north end.

"Kayla? Kayla? I asked if you could call Aaron and bring him up to speed on the application details," he says. "It would really help us land the account."

Before I answer, I quickly count to ten. When Liam

demands, my instinct is to say yes immediately. However, I have learned in recent months to pause before responding, ensuring my answer reflects my true feelings rather than a knee-jerk response.

"No, Liam, I won't call Aaron. He worked with me on the One Stop project and gained a lot of valuable experience. Also, after I gave my notice, I spent two weeks handing everything over to him. He should be across this, and you need to trust him. And if you can't trust him, hire someone else."

"Come on, Kayla. You know you're not actually going to leave—you love the hustle and bustle and pressure of the job too much. Besides, you're still on payroll for the next couple of weeks while you work out your holidays."

My hands ball into fists as I wonder if Liam ever really knew me at all. I never enjoyed working at the software development company he runs for his father. In fact, I should have resigned years ago. He could have picked that up from my resignation letter, if he'd bothered to read it.

There's no point in letting him know I got paid for my vacation days when I left my job either. He won't listen. My best plan is to stand strong. As my mind wanders, Liam carries on in my ear, equal parts cajoling and demanding. I imagine him sitting in his office overlooking Sydney Harbour, feet on his desk, confident he'll get his way. Well, not this time.

"Liam, I don't work for you and I won't be back. Aaron and Zuzu are fully capable of managing the new projects and addressing your concerns."

My eyes drift to the foamy waves lapping the sun kissed

beach. If only I could be out there now, strolling through the cool water, enjoying myself like that family playing in the breakers. I'm distracted by a tall male figure in running gear, loping along a path adjacent to the cove, and I take a moment to admire his form as Liam drones on.

What am I doing, letting Liam waste my time? This is one reason I left my job!

I'd said my last goodbyes and walked away from Avant-Garde two hours ago. Exhilarated at finally leaving that world behind, I'd jumped into my already loaded car and driven straight here, anticipation of my beach retreat giving me wings.

Even though I'd arrived fifteen minutes ago, I'd yet to set foot on the sand, let alone see the cottage I've rented for the next two months. I've made the break, but here I am still talking work with Liam. Enough is enough.

I tune back in as Liam switches gear onto us.

"If you're positive about leaving for good, we should give our relationship another chance," he says.

"What?" Before my mind catches up, the word tumbles out, leaving a heavy ache of regret in my chest. It would have been better to change the subject or to close him down. No, I'd given him an opening to carry on because I wasn't listening.

"We made a great team. I only broke up with you because we were so close, and that made things awkward at work."

Crossing my arms over my chest, I huff. The nerve of him. While I wasn't planning our wedding or anything, we had been getting quite serious. Suddenly, right before our one-year anniversary, Liam called it quits.

I thought I was heartbroken, but turns out I didn't miss him that much at all. In the end, he'd done me a favour. By letting me go he'd shown me much I'd lived in his shadow.

With him being absent from my personal life, and the project I'd been running for two years moving into a new phase, it was the kick in the pants I needed to leave the job I hated.

I'd fallen into the work after university. Liam had convinced me to try out working for him when we crossed paths at a University career day. With my creativity and design skills and his IT knowledge, he had me believing we'd be unstoppable.

It was supposed to be a stopgap while I searched for my dream job. Every time I'd tried to leave, Liam would convince me to stay a little longer. In three years I will be thirty, and when I celebrate that milestone I want to be doing something with my life that I'm proud of—something that brings me some measure of pleasure.

"Kayla? Kayla?"

"Sorry, Liam, what was that?"

"I said, come back to Sydney. Let's celebrate Christmas together with my family. You can head back to your beach retreat after if you want to."

That isn't going to happen. Partly because I've rented out my apartment for twelve months, so I've nowhere to stay. But mostly because I don't want to.

My phone rings. The screen shows it's my brother calling.

"Liam, my brother's ringing. I've gotta go. I'll be out of

touch except for emergencies now for the next month. Let's talk after that."

I cut the conversation before Liam can respond and accept Declan's call.

"Hi, Declan. How's the holiday going?"

My ears fill with the giggles of my two nieces for the first couple of seconds.

"Girls, can you give me a minute?"

And a minute is exactly what Declan gets. He has enough time to say, "Hi, Kayla," before their laughter starts up again, although it's muted enough for us to talk.

"We just dropped Mum and Dad off at the ship and we're on our way to the Gold Coast. Is it bad to say their deciding to go on a cruise for a month is the best Christmas present? The girls are so excited. They can't wait to hit the theme parks."

I grin as my nieces cheer in the background. "Yep, it was a great idea. I have to admit, I can't wait to get onto the beach."

Initially, I hadn't felt that way—we'd always celebrate Christmas as a family. Dad insisted he was taking Mum away as a thank you for putting up with him through a busy year, and I'd kept my mouth shut.

A week later, once I'd handed in my notice, I appreciated the gift of a family free break and had booked myself into a little cottage. Now, I get an entire month to myself to recharge my batteries and make sure I'm completely over the after-effects of Liam.

I've booked in an extra month after, so that when Mum and Dad are back and start asking about my future, I'll be far enough away not to feel the pressure of their expectations while I search for work.

"I'd better sort out the gaggle in the back. Just wanted to let you know the oldies are safely on their way. Love you."

"Love you."

I flick my phone off, and close my eyes, concentrating on the sound of the waves and the birds chirping, allowing nature to wash away the stress of the city and my high-pressure, low-satisfaction career, and the man who had been so much a part of my world.

"Hi, are you Kayla?" A cheery voice interrupts my peace.

My eyes snap open, and I try to focus on a lanky brown-haired woman looking through the open window, her blue eyes sparkling in welcome.

"Ah, yes. And you're Barb?"

"I am. Welcome to Cove Beach Houses. I was wondering if you were going to get out of the car, or turn around and go back to Sydney." Her laugh sounds forced.

"Sorry. I had a work call."

Barb cocks her head to the side as if she's studying me. "Oh? From what I overheard when I first came out to greet you, it sounded a bit more personal. Something about Christmas plans?"

For a second I'm lost for words. I'm not used to people admitting they've overheard my conversations. "Ah, he was my boyfriend until recently."

Barb winks. "So he's still chasing?"

I really don't know how to respond to that. We've just met, and I don't want to share my whole complicated Liam history with a stranger. Time for a change of subject. "He...

um…, I'm not sure what he wants. Anyway, I'm leaving Sydney behind for a while, and that includes Liam."

Her face splits into a huge, infectious grin. "Well, we can certainly help you escape. Let me show you round."

She steps back so I can exit the car. The air outside is warm, but the breeze from the ocean makes it bearable. I grab a suitcase from the boot, and Barb takes the other one, placing it on the ground.

"The cottage in front of you is mine," she says, pointing to a single-storey house giving off a Christmas vibe with lights strung around the doorway and an array of Christmas gnomes in the garden.

"I'm in most days, and I'm happy to help with local advice and such. I have occasional get togethers over the holidays, which you're welcome to join or not, as you wish. The first is tomorrow evening to welcome you and the Fawleys." Her arm sweeps out and gestures to the sea where the family is frolicking in the waves.

"They arrived yesterday, and have the end cottage on the right. Like you, they've taken a longer let, and will be here until after New Year. He's a doctor from England, and they're having a beach holiday before heading up to Armidale and a new life in Australia."

I nod, wondering how the Fawleys feel about having their life history discussed with a complete stranger. I also make a mental note to watch how much I tell Barb about why I'm here lest she over-share with others.

"The cottage beside mine is empty at the moment. Sam and Justine have been renting it Christmas and New Year's weeks since the cottages were built, way before I bought them. Sometimes their kids and grandkids come up for a few days, so they like the bigger unit beside me."

When I had booked last minute, Barb had been keen to point out the unit was only available this late in the year because it was a small, two-bedroom cottage used mainly for over-flow from the other two houses.

"Your place is down here," Barb says, starting off along a tree-lined path to a wooden building tucked away at the edge of the bush. Peeking out from behind it is another slightly larger beach house.

"I thought you only had the three rentals," I say, unreasonably annoyed about sharing my piece of paradise with anyone.

Barb laughs. "That's not one of mine. It's the MacIntosh place. They built their holiday home when the other houses went up, that's why they are so similar. Their son owns it now. He lives here full time, although he keeps pretty much to himself."

Creepy.

"You may see him out running, though," Barb adds.

My mind goes immediately to the guy in running gear I'd seen earlier, and I hope he isn't actually creepy.

"You might get to meet him tomorrow night, but definitely when Sam and Justine arrive. Their families have known each other since he was in short pants."

Barb ushers me onto the covered deck at the front of the cottage.

"Remember to introduce yourself to Fraser. He's not only my backup when I'm out, but it could be awkward living this close together for the next couple of months without knowing each other.

Given my reasons for being here, I'm uncertain about meeting the good-looking guy from next door. I don't want anything distracting me from my goals.

Fraser

The galley of my book tugs at my conscience as I stretch before my run.

"Sorry, but I can only do so much proof reading before the words jump over the page," I say out loud, in a last-ditch attempt to purge my guilt.

Running along the beach path, I consider turning back. It's Friday, and the galley is due at the publisher on Monday, and there's a sizeable chunk to do.

Through the trees I glimpse a woman sitting in a blue hatchback, head against the headrest, eyes closed, talking to herself. No, probably not to herself—most likely she's talking hands free on a phone. She's alone in the car, so I guess she's the person Barb mentioned is renting the cottage closest to mine.

I turn to run parallel to the beach. As I negotiate the track, I send a prayer to whoever is listening that she's not one of those people constantly talking on the phone. Sound travels far around here, and I have a lot of work to finish before my upcoming signing tour next month. It's not just the proofs, but the proposal for a new book, and critiquing six first chapters from students in the online crime writing for beginners course I teach.

My feet pound the sandy path, each footstep another arrow piercing my conscience. When I wrote news for the ABC website, deadlines were strict, and editing as I wrote was essential. Why do these same activities seem like a waste of time now that I write fiction? Is it the drive to always be creating?

Half an hour in, I'm loosening up and the stress is leaving my shoulders. Cutting down a track to the beach, I turn around. Closer to home, I'm so engrossed in blocking out the world, I almost topple one of the kids staying in the holiday lets. I place the girl back on her feet, add an apology, then head off again.

Making my way up the pathway between the group of houses, I nod hello to Barb as she makes her way to the car to greet the newcomer. I watch as she greets the woman, startling her a little from her reaction, then makes way as she gets out of the car. As she does, I make a quick assessment; late twenties, professional dress highlighting a curvy figure. What captures my attention is the mass of red hair tumbling free to her shoulders—I'm a sucker for a redhead.

My toe stubs a rock and I stumble. *Mind on the path,* I remind myself. *A sprained ankle would be a pain over Christmas.*

While I warm down, I remind myself of something else. *Dude, you know how holiday flings work out, so don't even think about it. Give your heart a break and keep your distance from her.*

I'm standing under the shower when I catch bits and pieces of a conversation through the bathroom window. It's Barb's usual patter outlining the amenities provided in the small cottage. By the time I'm drying off, she is reminding the woman about the mixer tomorrow night.

"It's pot luck, so bring a little something to eat and drink."

Damn, I forgot about tomorrow. Sam and Justine won't be here yet, but I'm almost certain Barb will come find me if I don't appear to greet her new guests, especially as they're all going to be here over the Christmas break. It isn't just that, as the only permanent residents here, we like to support each other. It's also because, traditionally, Christmas at the cottages has been a shared experience and Barb likes to keep that going.

My family came here for Christmas every year when I was a kid. There were a couple of other families who did the same, and we made a big thing about festive activities. We always welcomed anyone else who was staying and wanted to be part of it.

While some families drifted apart as we grew up, Mum and Dad continued to visit for Christmas. If I could, I would join them.

When Barb bought the other four aging properties here and rehabbed them using the money from her divorce, my parents inducted her into the cove's festive traditions. I believe they helped her get through a difficult time in her life that first Christmas, and the experience stayed with her.

My parents died in a car accident a couple of years after. A little later, when I moved here to grieve, and to finish my first Harry Carpenter book, Barb had returned the favour and seen me through my grief. When the estate was winding up, I'd used the proceeds from my book advance and my savings to buy my sister's half of the cottage.

In the five years since, Barb and I have become good friends, always looking out for each other. I help her fend off the men who believe they can change her life. And, last year, when I'd fallen head over heels for a renter, Barb had picked up the pieces when the woman left me behind without a second thought.

I'd turned thirty last month, and Barb had shared a whiskey or two with me as I took stock of my life. It's a privilege to write full time. I don't even mind too much doing the writer festival circuit, or the fact I have to teach writing to make ends meet. However, I am self-aware enough to know I'm in a rut.

I grab an iced tea, head to the deck, and stare blankly at the galley pages of the fifth Harry Carpenter novel. I identify strongly with the tenacious journalist who investigates crimes, and makes the world a better place by exposing the underbelly of London society. Readers lap him up too. Sighing, I sit down and push the pages away, unable to face more proofreading today. It's not that I don't enjoy writing the stories, it's more that writing a book a year for the same series, for five years, has become almost too formulaic. The challenge is gone.

I pull my laptop towards me. Doing a bit of admin work before dinner is a good alternative. Front and centre is a notification for an email I've been waiting for from my agent. What's inside could be the difference between getting by as a full-time writer and having enough income to choose my own projects.

My mouse hovers over the link—I'm almost too scared to open it. Wishing I'd grabbed a beer instead of tea, I take the plunge and click. Immediately I wish I hadn't. Why isn't anything in life easy?

> Fraser, while Paul is interested in turning Harry Carpenter into a television series, they usually like to have 8-10 books on the shelves before picking up a new author.
>
> I spoke with the publishers, and they are keen to sign you up for another five books over five years, especially as that will tie in with the studio deal.
>
> Let's talk about this when we meet next week.
>
> Phil

I re-read the email and my heart sinks. Most authors would give their right arm for a five book deal and a potential television series. All I see is another tie to Harry Carpenter. He pays the bills, but he's not a passion project any more.

I sigh, and swallow the last of my drink, before heading down to the beach to remind myself how lucky I am that I live here and make a reasonable living. Perhaps the sea air will allow me to get a grip on reality and inspire me with a new idea for Harry Carpenter number six.

CHAPTER 2
YEAH, BEACH BUM

Kayla

Barb is not at all what I expected from a rental host. She is so open and friendly, and she treats her guests like a little community. It wasn't what I wanted when I planned a beach escape, but I'm sure I can be sociable on the odd evenings so long as I get the rest of the time to myself.

I trundle the cases into the master bedroom at the back of the house, although "master bedroom" is a grand name for the slightly larger of the two small double rooms. They're both decorated in cheery blues and whites, with exposed wooden floors and painted wooden furniture. Opening the curtain, I find it looks out into a small backyard, with neatly trimmed grass and a border of Waratahs hiding the wooden fence. I'm pleased to see there's a washing line too and an outdoor shower head, essential for washing the beach off before entering the cottage.

After unpacking, I slip the suitcases under the bed and

take my toiletries into the bathroom. The bathroom also contains a linen closet, which has a washing machine tucked into a space in the bottom. Opposite the bathroom is the toilet, which shares a wall with the master bedroom. Good thing I'm here by myself, as the old unit looks like it could be pretty noisy to flush.

I close the hallway door to the bedrooms behind me as I return to the living area. Barb has assured me I can reorganise things in here if I want to. She even said I should get Fraser from next door to lend a hand when he's not working.

To my left is a lounge area with a sofa bed facing a small TV, that I am assured has all the usual apps and the ABC channels. To my right is a kitchenette with an island bar. Dead centre in the room is a big wooden table surrounded by four wooden chairs. I check the light and decide not to change anything yet.

Before I head out to get the rest of my things from the car, I open the fridge to make sure my food delivery was stowed appropriately. Not only does the local supermarket do online ordering and home delivery, for an extra charge they put it away for you. I open the cupboards to see what staples have come with the rental. Satisfied I will only need some fresh food top ups while I'm here, I make my way up the path to the car.

My first trip I take down the two large carry bags from my shopping expedition last weekend. The smaller of the two I leave on the table. The other, heavier one, I take over to the sofa and unpack my book haul. I've been so busy over the last two years I haven't read a single book, and I aim to make up for that over the next eight weeks.

My selection includes fantasy and sci-fi books, some graphic novels, and a couple of chick lit books I've been dying to read. I organise them on the shelf under the TV, and tidy the bag away into the pantry to be used again later.

Then I bring in the last of my luggage—a cardboard box containing my holiday project that I plonk onto the table. I drop onto a chair and catch my breath before unpacking the box.

First out is my watercolour easel. Battered and sporting the scars of previous projects, I place it at the end of the table, where I can move it around to capture the light. Beside it, I add a selection of ceramic flower pallets, a couple of glass jars, and my paint box, before sliding the cardboard box down the other end of the table.

Next, I empty the second bag, spraying out a selection of watercolour paints and brushes. It has been so long since I painted, I had little worth salvaging from the stuff I had in storage. So, I went shopping, and I bought everything new in an effort to inspire myself to get back into what had once been my passion. Finally, I remove the specially cut sheets of watercolour paper and look for somewhere to keep them safe.

As I do, I catch sight of the runner I'd seen earlier. Through the sliding doors to the desk, I watch my neighbour walk along the path to the beach. Dressed in shorts, t-shirt and thongs, he moves with the ease of a natural athlete. When he reaches the sand he half turns, looking back my way, then raises an arm, and I think he's going to wave hello.

My breath hitches as I glance away, my pulse quickening with a silent plea to go unnoticed. I'm not ready to make friends yet. Before I indulge myself in getting to know the neighbours, I want to settle in, find a routine, and focus on recapturing my dreams.

Watching him from the corner of my eye as I rummage through my things, I catch him running a hand through dark curly hair, and I wonder if he even saw me, he appears so lost in his own thoughts. He turns back towards the water before meandering down to the edge of the sea, and wonder if it might have been nice if he *had* said hello.

I shake that thought from my head—remember the plan. I'm all too aware of how a fling can turn into something more. A supposed one-night stand with Liam on a work trip showed me the folly of thinking that way. Having finally broken free of his clutches, I want to centre myself and be certain of my own plans before starting anything with anyone else. Slipping the watercolour paper back into the bag, I place the bundle behind the sofa for safe keeping before making my way through the other things in the cardboard box.

Inside are the remnants of one of my uni projects. Our task had been to paint character designs for a movie, TV series, or book, along with a full character break down to show how we'd incorporated their characteristics into the final product. I had gone one further and imagined my own graphic novel. My intention had been to finish it one day. Well, today is the day.

I remove my laptop bag, place it on the table, then pick up the exercise book with the story outline and flick through it. Okay, maybe tomorrow is the day—I can take one evening to be a beach bum.

Deciding I need to unwind a bit from the journey, I head for the kitchen and pour myself a gin and tonic over ice, then remove a pre-prepared antipasto platter, and pop everything on a tray. Grabbing a book from the top of the pile, I take my haul out to the deck. After placing the tray on the coffee table, I eye the two chairs and sofa in the deck setting. Choosing the sofa option, I make myself comfortable and open the book.

It has been so long since I've had the time to just sit and read, but I'm soon blocking out the world as I lose myself in the story. Some part of me notices the guy next door come back from his walk along the beach, but not even he can take me out of the fantasy world I've jumped into.

Fraser

Sitting in the soft sand close by the path, I watch the sky darken over the water as the sun sets behind me. All the while, I run different scenarios through my head. Without the show deal, would the publisher have wanted to sign me up for more books? And the director wants a guarantee of more books before he'll talk with me. "I'm trapped on the hamster wheel of my success," I say to the waves.

Flopping back on the sand, I watch the stars appear in the sky. I'd always wanted to be a writer. Since childhood I'd escaped into imaginary worlds at every opportunity, either reading or writing stories.

After high school I'd gone to uni and done a combined journalism and creative writing degree, knowing journalism was my best chance at getting paid, but not able to give up on my dream of becoming an author.

When I had turned up to a pitch day six years ago, it had been on a dare. Friends had read my writing attempts, and they called me out for not trying to get published. Goaded into action, I'd turned up with my synopsis and the first few chapters of my dream book, a historic whodunnit. The agent I saw liked the idea, but more importantly, he liked my style.

Unfortunately, even though the story idea was sound, Phil said he couldn't sell it in the current market. Then he'd asked if I had any other options. I had been experimenting with a modern whodunnit crime solving reporter, and he encouraged me to work that up for him.

Over the next couple of weeks, I'd worked on a pitch in my spare time and sent it through. Two months later he'd come back with a deal from an international publisher. They would take it if I changed the setting—Australia was too small a market. They wanted me to move everything to the UK. I'd compromised, and Harry Carpenter became an Aussie journo in London.

The first book had been difficult. I'd relied on google maps, the internet, and a superb editor to get the look and feel of my guy in England right. After the success of the first book, the publisher had flown me over for some events, and I got to do some in person research. The second book was even better. Now I have a readership with an insatiable appetite for Harry Carpenter stories.

"Oh, quit whinging," I tell myself. "There is a way around

this. You could take a risk, give up the teaching for a year, and try to put out two books in your time off."

At the thought of losing an income stream, my hands go clammy and I feel like I can't breathe. The last year has taught me that financial security is precarious. My younger sister lost her job ten months ago, and was finding it difficult to get another that fitted in with bringing up two children and running a household. Even though her husband was working all the hours he could, they had been on the verge of losing their home.

I'd been able to loan them some money to tide them over, but it had taken most of my savings. With my current income, I can pay the bills with a little left over for the occasional luxury, but until Isla's back on her feet and can repay me, I can't take the risk.

"Suck it up, prince," I tell myself. It's not like I hate my job. I get to work here, I love writing, and I make okay money. I'll give it a couple of years and then revisit where I am. If I have my savings back, perhaps I'll be able to pause the teaching and take a year to write my other novel while I'm editing the Harry Carpenter one.

The smell of barbecue meat wafts past me and my stomach rumbles. Pushing myself to my feet, I shake the sand off before making my way back up the beach path.

My new neighbour is stuck in a book, and I bite back a sigh. I hope she's not a fan. This is my safe space. I like to leave the public face for the book signings and literary festivals. She shifts and I catch sight of the cover. It reeks of fantasy. I don't know whether to feel relieved or appalled— she's not a real reader after all.

And is that supermarket pre-prepared antipasto? Mum would turn in her grave if I did that! Through the door to the living room, it looks like some painting stuff set up on the table inside. So, an amateur painter who reads fantasy, probably fantasy romance.

"Dodged a bullet there, boy," I mutter as I open the deck door. She's gorgeous, hot even, but so not my type, which is good because I don't need a repeat of last year.

I make a quick risotto and take it and a white wine to the table on the deck, determined to finish the last checks of my galley. On the table, my phone buzzes. It's a text from Isla.

> Last chance to save me. If you're
> not coming for Christmas, then
> we're off to Dean's parents' on
> Sunday.

> Sorry sis. Book stuff.

I hate lying. Well, stretching the truth is more like it. I do have to meet with Phil next week to sort my contracts, so I wouldn't be able to leave until after that. Then it would be a long drive up to Brisbane to make it for Christmas Day. Besides, I'm going to be up there late January, anyway.

> We'll be together next year, I
> promise.

While I eat my dinner, I check another twenty pages, then settle down to read the first chapter from one of the six writers doing my online course. I force myself to finish it. It's horrible. There's always one writer in each course who thinks they know better—a know-it-all who breaks the rules of writing before they understand why you need them.

Finishing the chapter, I review my notes, wondering how best to structure the criticism. I'm distracted by a light going on next door. From my position on the deck, I can see through a small side window into the living area.

Light bounces off my new neighbour's auburn hair, creating a halo of colour that appeals to the Scots side of my Scottish/Italian heritage. Distracted from my work, I watch her move confidently about the kitchen as she prepares her dinner, then she crosses the room and closes the blind. Did she catch me staring? My cheeks heat, then I chuckle.

"She probably thinks you're a creep," I tell myself. "Good thing you aren't really interested in her." And even if I was, she wouldn't have anything to do with some weird guy who watches her cook.

"And that's good, mate, because the last thing you need is a fling with a renter—especially not in the middle of some critical negotiations."

With that thought, I open my laptop and create a new document and stretch my creative abilities as I craft a tactful chapter assessment for my student.

CHAPTER 3
YO, BEACH VIBES

Kayla

Waking up to birdsong rather than an alarm is new. I stretch under the covers and study the bright blue sky through a chink in the curtains. For the first time in—I don't know how long—I slept through the night. It could have something to do with the fact I switched off my phone. Or maybe it was because I didn't put my book down until I'd finished it.

Now I'm awake and energised. I quickly dress in shorts and a t-shirt and pad out to the kitchen. Opening the deck door, I let in the warm sea breeze and stretch again. If switching off for one night has me feeling this good, I should have done it years ago.

A quick study of the fridge and I decide on muesli, yoghurt, and berries for breakfast. I put the kettle on and pop a tea bag in a cup, then load up a bowl. My phone eyes me from the counter. I told Declan I'd check my phone morning and night. It can wait until after breakfast, though.

I take my tray onto the deck, then nip back in and grab a sketch pad and pencils. The view from my cottage is too good to miss in the early morning light. As I sketch and eat, I watch the world wake up.

After cleaning my dishes, I turn on my phone. There's a photo from Declan of the kids on the beach last night. I send a heart. There are a couple of messages from Liam. I can see from the display they're about work. Without a second thought I delete them. Powering down my phone, I grab my beach bag and drawing stuff, and head for the sand.

Finding a comfy spot in the shade of a tree, I set myself up with a view of kids playing and start trying some new character sketches for my novel. My hand flies over the paper, joy running through my veins as I'm finally creating again.

I've been there for about an hour when the guy from next door runs past. I avert my eyes as he passes, but as he reaches the water's edge, I take a quick peek to find he's wearing board shorts and nothing else. When he jumps in the water to swim, I can't help but see how fit and toned his body is.

As he dives through the breakers and swims out to the headland, I stop drawing and take time to admire his form as he cuts through the waves, the athletic version of my neighbour seeming at odds with the cute academic I'd watched last night. His head was bent over some papers, all his attention focused on what he was doing. He must have felt something because he'd looked up, and I immediately turned and busied myself in the kitchen. I'd given it a few minutes, then

I closed the blinds. I didn't want him to think I was some sort of stalker.

As if it has a mind of its own, my pencil outlines a figure with the same lithe proportions as my neighbour. When he disappears from view, I turn my attention to adding detail to my study from memory, making sure I capture his slightly too long wavy hair, and those dark eyes framed by those amazing lashes. *He'd make such a great hero for my book.* I roll the idea around in my mind as I add armour and weapons to my fantasy version of a man I'd yet to even speak to.

I'm so engrossed, I don't notice anyone approach until a shadow falls over my pad. My first thought is it's my new neighbour returning from his swim, and I surreptitiously cover the picture of him I'm working on. However, when I turn my head, I find a tall, fair-haired woman in her mid-thirties leaning over and watching me draw.

It's the mother of the kids playing in the ocean. If she's here, then who's looking after them? I glance up to find my neighbour has finished his swim and is playing some sort of ball game with the children.

"You've a knack for this." The woman grins cheekily.

"I.., I'm." Embarrassment floods through me and my face heats, not a good thing for a redhead as my cheeks will advertise my mortification at being caught drawing a complete stranger. My brain frantically searches for words, unable to find any before the woman rescues me.

"I'm Alice Frawley. We have the rental on the end over there." The woman points to the largest of the beach houses before returning her eyes to the water.

"Hi, I'm Kayla Harrison, artist in residence," I joke. "Or at least trying to be."

"I'd say you're more than trying. That's actually a pretty good likeness, although I'm not sure I would have imagined Fraser wielding a sword."

"I'm..., um...,"

She drops beside me and pats my arm. "No need to explain, Kayla. We all have our fantasies, and he's definitely worth fantasising over."

My laugh sounds a little forced. "I'm not fantasising about him..., well at least not that way." Although I could if I'd let myself. "It's for a fantasy style novel I'm toying with. I was sketching ideas when he came by and this image popped into my head."

"Oh," Alice says, sounding unconvinced.

Feeling the need to prove myself, I flip the page over and show the drawing I did of her kids. The oldest girl is an elf, the middle child, a boy, I've turned into a goblin, and the youngest is a sort of fairy or pixie—I'll have to go back through the characters to jog my memory. "They're all characters from my book," I explain.

"Actually, in all seriousness, that's very cool. How would you draw me?"

I study her for a bit. "There isn't anyone like you in the book, but if I was going to have someone...,"

My hand moves of its own accord, and in a few minutes I have the outline of a mature warrior princess. You can see the weariness in her bones, but the determination to carry on in her stance and her eyes.

Beside me, Alice laughs. "Wow, that looks like me at the end of a shift in A&E."

"You're a nurse?"

"Yes, I am. And some days when I finish up, it certainly feels like I've fought battle after battle."

"Good morning, ladies."

With my sketch book wide open and my artistic vulnerability exposed, of course, that deep voice belongs to my neighbour, who has appeared beside Alice. I curse my fair complexion as my face heats. And if I'm not feeling guilty enough for drawing complete strangers, at the moment a gust of wind flicks the pages of my pad open to that drawing of him.

I quickly close the sketch pad and glance up in time to see his lips twitch into an almost smile.

"Fraser, have you met Kayla yet?" Alice asks, rescuing me from certain embarrassment.

"No, I haven't had the pleasure." Fraser's voice is almost a purr that sends tingles through every nerve in my body.

"Hi," I say, surprised I can get that one word out. I'm so off balance.

"Hi," he says back, his gaze holding mine.

"Will we see you at the get together tonight, Fraser?" Alice asks, and Fraser's smile lights up his face before he turns to Alice.

"I wouldn't miss it for the world."

My heart skips a beat as he sends a side glance my way. I lower my gaze, but I follow his progress up the path through lowered lashes.

Alice nudges me. "Pity he won't be on the menu, eh?"

Before I can think of a witty response, she stands and brushes the sand from her shorts. "Duty calls. See you later."

Fraser

I can't wipe the grin from my face as I head back home. She was so checking me out. That drawing proves it. I chuckle. Even if she drew me a bit on the skinny side, I kinda like myself as a warrior.

My mother would have called it lanky, like she used to when she told me, incorrectly, that I'd fill out when I got older. I've come to terms with my body. Still, it would have been better for my ego if she had bulked me up a little, especially as I was carrying a badass sword.

My first instinct had been to tease her about drawing me. Then she'd coloured a deep scarlet under that dusting of freckles. So, I'd bitten back my admiring comments and allowed myself to feel silently flattered. Then I thought how much I hoped she'd be going to the get together tonight, before clamping that thought firmly down—once bitten and all that.

As I turn on the kettle, I repeat: fantasy romance, supermarket antipasto, holiday let. I've dropped the amateur artist because she's clearly very good—and I'm not just saying that because of the picture of me.

Even after repeating this a few times, I still turn the shower to cold while I wash off the sand from my swim.

There is something about that girl—I can't get her out of my head.

I take my coffee out to my work table on the deck and try to concentrate on finishing the proofs for my book. It's meticulous, tedious work and, after an hour or so, I need a break. I decide to assess another student's first chapter, but not before I've made a fresh pot of coffee.

Flicking through the other chapters, I choose one that I at least think will be promising. If I have a star student in this course, she's the one. The writing is concise and introduces the main characters and setting in a way that draws me in. Still, nothing is completely perfect, and there are ways that my student can make her work even better. While I draft out some notes, I'm hyper-aware that my new neighbour is still sitting on the beach, still sketching.

She is alone now. About half an hour ago, I heard a car leave, telling me the family renting the end house have gone out, hopefully for the rest of the day, allowing me to get on with my work without distractions.

The woman on the beach stands and stretches. I can't take my eyes off her. Okay, noisy kids are not the only thing that might distract me from my work. How can she be so quiet and still be able to intrude into my work bubble?

I duck my head down as she comes back up the path to her cottage. The last thing I want is for her to catch me staring at her—again. It will give her completely the wrong idea. My phone pings, but I wait until she is out of view before picking up the text. It's from Isla.

> Worried about you working and
> being alone. Come join us.

Part of me desperately wants to be with Isla and her family for Christmas, but the biggest part of me wishes they had been able to come here. Cove Beach is where we used to celebrate with Mum and Dad, and it still oozes Christmas for me. Normally they come down every alternate year, but Isla only recently told me they couldn't afford it this year.

Because it had been my year for Christmas, I had planned to be here, and had even organised a book signing tour in Queensland a couple of weeks later so I could spend a little extra time with my nephews over the holidays. By the time I'd realised they weren't coming down, it had been too late to change things.

I'll be fine.

I have friends, the beach, and I have books.

Thought you might say that.

I laugh.

You know me so well.

Sooooo, we're sending you an early Christmas present. Are you home tomorrow?

I'm out for the morning markets, but otherwise I'll be here.

Good, it will arrive around 10.
Love you

I place the phone back on the table and check under the poinsettia plant I have in place of a tree. Yep, there's a gift there from Isla and Dean, and it's pretty obviously a book. How odd they're giving me something else.

My stomach rumbles and I check the time on my laptop. If I break for lunch now, I'll get another couple of hours work in this afternoon before getting ready for the party tonight.

The Italian goodies I purchased for tonight's platter occupy most of the space inside my fridge. The thought of antipasto draws my mind back to my neighbour and her supermarket platter.

I sneak a glance through the window above the sink. From here it looks like she's going through some papers in a box, and maybe organising them on the table. I shake my head. *Come on, Fraser, I know it's been a while, but she's just a woman.*

Determined to put the cute redhead from my mind, I grab some bread and make a sandwich before going back out on the deck to finish proofing the galley before Barb's gathering.

Kayla

My hands shake with nervous anticipation as I sort through the papers in the carton. I'm excited to be delving back into my novel, but I was also nervous; worried that my idea wasn't as good as I remembered.

Most of the papers are original sketches and outlines for all the main characters that I'd handed in for my project. I'd also drafted outlines for the lesser characters. Ooh, there's the map I scribbled out for the fantasy world they live in. Finally, there is the notebook where I'd outlined the story.

The bunch of papers at the bottom are where I'd come unstuck. I had attempted to storyboard the book, but as I'd progressed, I'd found the story quite boring. It wasn't something I'd ever read. Then I'd had finals and the post-uni job hunt. Soon after, I was working what felt like all day, every day, and the carton had been in the back of my wardrobe for years now.

After a morning of sketching and relaxing, I feel ready to attack my project and revisit the tale. However, before I get too involved, I have to work out what I'm going to take to the party tonight.

With my home delivery, I'd included eggs and bacon and butter. When I'd checked the cupboards yesterday, I'd found the cottage basics included flour and salt. Among the pots and pans I find a baking dish the right size for my mum's bacon and egg pie.

Although my stomach protests about not being dealt with first, I make the pastry for the pie and put it in the fridge to rest before throwing together a salad for lunch. Along with my plate, I take the book with my storyline and a pen out onto the deck. As I eat, I review and take notes on the changes I'm planning to make.

The basic story idea is still sound; a young boy whose

magic allows him to blend into the shadows is taken from his home to train as a spy for the king. His training mate is a girl who, although small in stature, is deadly with weapons and poisons. The other main character was the king's right-hand man, who is also the spymaster. I have two new ones to add after this morning—a female warrior who teaches them combat skills, and the Captain of the King's Guard, who is also part of the spy network and takes the fledgling spies under his wing.

The original book had been my hero's origin story, but, in my head, this was the first book in a series. Then I'd realised most of the characters would only be in this book and I'd have to create new ones to carry the series. This time, I want to use that as background and concentrate on my spies' first solo mission, which was where the last story ended.

By the time I've finished eating, I'm ready to start on version two of my tale, but I make the pie first. When it's in the oven, I pull out a fresh notebook and start writing the tale scene by scene. I only stop to take the pie out and to make myself a cup of tea. The speed the story flows takes me by surprise. Then again, it has been five years in the making.

Picking up some sketching paper, I start a rough story-board. I lose track of time until a car pulls up in the carpark and Alice calls out, "Come on kids, we're running late."

From my position at the table, I can't make out the clock on the oven, so I open my laptop to find I've only got about half an hour before Barb's get-together.

After putting my work away, I turn on the kettle and make some tea, then put it in the fridge to cool. I rush through showering, and pull on an orange retro patterned shift dress and flat sandals, then run a comb through my hair. Picking up my makeup bag, I study myself in the mirror, then pop it back down—I don't need to impress anyone.

When I check my laptop, I have five minutes to spare. Just enough time to use the tea to make a gin cocktail for the adults, and to arrange the pie on a plate. I used to love this pie when I was a kid, and I hope Alice's tribe enjoys it.

Fortunately, my speedy clothes change means I'm only a little late, but the sound of conversation from Barb's deck tells me at least the Frawley family arrived before me.

"Ah, Kayla, you came." Barb kisses my cheek, takes my pie and swirls away; her magenta maxi-dress creating a splash of colour in the evening light as she takes it over to the food table.

White fairy lights decorate the deck, and in the corner is an artistic natural wood Christmas tree. Each thin eucalyptus branch protrudes at right angles from the centre stem, cut and arranged to mimic the traditional cone shape. Hanging off each limb is a Christmas gnome or a red bauble.

As I admire the tree, Alice joins me, a round-faced, middle-aged man in tow. "Hon, it looks like Kayla brought cocktails."

"Excellent, gin too, by the smell. Shall I relieve you of that?" he says, taking the pitcher from me. He winks and adds, "I'll be back with glasses for everyone in a mo."

"That's Charles, by the way. Charles, this is Kayla."

We're soon settled on Barb's outdoor lounge furniture with drinks, and the kids have taken off to play some sort of tag game on the sand. The Frawleys are an easy-going couple and take over the conversation. Barb and I are content to listen and offer comments when asked questions.

"So when the opportunity came up to take a position in a GP practice in Australia, I jumped at it—especially when they assured me Alice should be able to get work easily enough too."

"Isn't it scary leaving your family behind and coming half-way around the world?" I ask.

Charles laughs. "My family is a nightmare. I'm happy to leave them behind. Alice not so much."

Alice's face twists into a grimace. "My dad passed away last year, and I hate leaving Mum behind. She pressed us to go though, and is excited about coming out for a visit some-time soon."

Charles slips an arm around his wife's waist and gives her a quick hug. "Enough about us. What is it you do, Kayla?"

"Nothing," I say, then giggle at their astonished faces. "Well, nothing at the moment. I've been working as a Project Manager for a web and app development company."

"Wow," Alice says. "High flying or what?"

I twirl my glass in my hand. "Sometimes it was quite intense, but I was so busy I hardly noticed."

"That's why she's come here. She wanted somewhere to chill out for a while," Barb tells everyone.

"I thought you were an artist or something this morning, with those cool pictures you were drawing," Alice says. "Didn't you mention something about writing a book?"

Although I've spent all day working on my novel, I suddenly feel strange talking about it. It's not like I'm an author, or artist, or anything. "I'm doing a graphic novel. It was an idea I had at uni. I shelved it but now I've got some time off, I thought I'd revisit it."

"How exciting and brave of you," Charles says.

"Not as brave as coming half-way round the world," I say.

Charles shrugs. "I don't know. You're putting something internal on paper. I've always admired people who can do that."

"It's not high literature or anything. It's just a graphic novel," I protest.

"You know our Fraser is an author. He even teaches classes. I'm sure he'd give you a few tips," Barb adds.

I've only ever shared my writings with my uni professor, and the thought of showing my stuff to someone who actually writes for a living has me paralysed. Not to mention the fact I've actually fantasised about including him in my story as a new character.

I can only imagine what he'd say about my scribblings. I'd be gutted if my sword-wielding hero cut me down. Besides, it's not like I'm wanting to get the book published or anything. I simply want to finish it.

Fraser

I pull into the carpark, grab my stuff, then rush down to the cottage. Pulling out the platter I set up earlier and a bottle of Prosecco I left cooling in the fridge, I'm ready to go.

As I head for the door, I catch sight of myself in the glass. Damn, Barb will be septic if I don't at least make a bit of an effort. I'm running late because I wanted to get the finished galley off to my publisher. The post box isn't emptied until tomorrow morning, but now I don't have to go into town before my weekly visit to the local markets. Besides, the thrill of having another book ready for publishing had energised me and I couldn't sit still—I simply had to send it on its way.

I pop everything back on the bench and nip into the bedroom. Changing my thongs for trainers, I then swap my Pink Floyd t-shirt for a plain white one before pulling a short-sleeved shirt over the top. A quick brush of my hair does little to tame my unruly locks. I frown at my image in the mirror—nothing short of a haircut will fix that mop.

Now, I'm really late. I rush over to Barb's place and turn the corner just in time to hear the cute neighbour say, "It's just a graphic novel."

Then, horror of horrors, Barb responds with, "You know our Fraser is an author. He even takes classes. I'm sure he'd give you a few tips."

I want to slink back round the corner and head for the hills. For so many reasons, giving writing advice to Kayla would be a bad idea, not least because I aim to avoid that woman invading my thoughts as much as possible while she's here.

"Ah, there you are, Fraser. I was just telling Kayla that you're a writer and you teach courses. I thought maybe you might like to help her with the book she's writing this Christmas."

My gaze drifts to Kayla and her face is a stricken mask,

which perfectly reflects my inner thoughts; although I hope I'm hiding it a little better. My head is telling me to make some excuse not to become involved because I really don't have either the time or inclination. On the other hand, my heart tells me Barb is simply doing what she always does, turning her renters into a little temporary family. She's too good a friend for me to reject her idea and make things awkward for her.

"Give me a minute," I say, trying to gather my thoughts while I place the platter down on the food table, and the wine in a chilli bin full of ice. I grab a beer and return to the group, professional writer face at the ready.

"Alice, Charles, Kayla, this is Fraser, our other local. Fraser, this is the Christmas crew."

"We've met already," Alice says as I raise my beer in a cheers motion.

A scuffle breaks out on the sand, where I assume the kids are playing, and Charles leaves to sort it out.

"Those monsters are Lottie, Joe and Ella," Alice says. "So, what do you write, Fraser?"

"I write crime fiction," I tell her.

Charles stops halfway up the stairs and stares at me, mouth open. "You're Fraser MacIntosh, aren't you? I love your books. Honey, you know the ones I mean. You bought the latest one for me to read on the plane."

"Charles is a bit of a crime nut," Alice says apologetically. "Are you him, though?"

"Yes," I say.

Charles is rocking backwards and forwards on his feet, as if he's going to say something, then stops as if he's not sure he should. "Is it true you have another book coming out? I mean, the last one's only been out a couple of months, but I heard there was another one in the pipeline?" he eventually asks.

I nod. "That's why I'm a little late. I wanted to post the final proofs to my publisher. This one should be out later next year."

"Cool. And is it true they're going to make a Harry Carpenter TV series?"

This isn't something I want to talk about, or even *can* talk about, given the state of negotiations. But I don't want to lie to him either, so I tap the side of my nose, letting him know the answer is a secret.

"Say no more," Charles grins, clearly pleased to have some sort of inside running.

There is an awkward silence, broken only by the children arriving clamouring for food. Charles and Alice take them over to the table and set them up with some pie and fizz, while Barb excuses herself to bring out a lasagne she is warming in the oven.

Kayla and I remain standing in the middle of the deck. She takes a sip of her drink and I say, "If you want some help with your book, I'll be—"

"Look, I know you're going to be polite, but you don't need to look at my stuff. It's not crime, and it's not really a book."

She's let me off the hook, and now I'm not sure I want to be. Part of it's the blow to my pride that she's not jumping at the chance to work with me, but, if I'm honest, it's also partially because I'm intrigued.

"I've never worked on a graphic novel, but I'd be happy to at least review your story structure."

"It's, um, fantasy."

"Story structure is story structure, no matter the genre."

"I thought most writers of other genres believe fantasy is a bit low brow," she says.

I blink a couple of times. Had she read my thoughts yesterday? I'm not trying to be a snob, but serious writers don't give fantasy much respect. However, I'm surprised I come across that way.

"I'm willing to give it a go if you are," I persist, my professional pride now really in danger of being dented.

She shrugs. "It's far from being ready for anyone else to read."

I clutch my chest. "You're rejecting my help? I'm gutted," I tease.

She smiles, and dimples appear. Right now she could ask anything of me and I'd fall over my feet to provide it.

"Maybe when I've done a little more work," she concedes.

For a moment, our eyes meet and I almost drown in their deep green pools. This woman is working some sort of spell on me, and I'm desperately trying to remember why getting to know her better is such a bad idea.

"Dinner's ready," Barb says, breaking the moment.

We wander over to the table and load our plates with food.

"This platter is so delicious," Kayla says to me. "I had to resort to a bland supermarket one from an online delivery last night, and bland is the nicest thing I can say about it."

"Everything here's from a local farmer's market."

"Please tell me they don't shut down for Christmas," she says, placing some salami on her plate.

"They do, but you're in luck. The last one for the year is tomorrow. I can take you if you like." The words are out of my mouth before my brain kicks into gear.

Those dimples appear again, and for a moment I forget why it's such a bad idea for me to spend time with Kayla. Catching sight of Barb's raised eyebrows, I remember the months it took me to get over my broken heart, and I regret inviting Kayla on my weekly shopping expedition.

Before I can retract my words, Kayla is saying, "Umm, okay. That would be great."

It won't be so bad, we can go as friends, no big deal, I try to convince myself as I lead Kayla over to join the others. We spend the next couple of hours chatting and eating. The night ends earlyish as the Frawleys leave to take their exhausted offspring to bed.

Not long after, I walk back with Kayla in companionable silence. As she turns off to her place, I say, "I'll come by about eight tomorrow morning."

"See you then."

Despite my concerns about getting too close to Kayla, there's a real spring in my step as I follow the path the rest of the way home.

CHAPTER 4
HEY, BEACH BUDDY

Kayla

Leaning my head against the glass of the sliding door, I watch Fraser disappear into the night. In an effort to calm my mind and my raging emotions, I draw in a deep breath and slowly let it out slowly.

There is no doubt being physically close to Fraser sends all sorts of hormones racing round by body, no matter how often I tell myself I'm not attracted to him. I'm all over the place, so I'm not sure how I actually feel about him taking a look at my story outline.

On the way to the bedroom, I stop by the table and rifle through the drawings and notes containing my ideas. My holiday project has now morphed into something serious that is going to be scrutinised by a published author, and a relatively famous one.

I've never read one of his books, but you'd have to be

braindead not to know about the journalist turned successful writer. Even worse, it appears his books are going to be made into a television series.

There's no way I can let him read my scribblings. It'd be mortifying watching him try to find something nice to say about them. And there's always the possibility he might feel the need to avoid me so he doesn't have to tell me how bad it is. And I don't want that.

Hold on, where did that come from?

He's cute, and good company, and I'm definitely attracted to him, but that's how things started with Liam. It was supposed to be a fling. Then he was organising every facet of my life. I didn't even have the strength to break away from him, not even when my mother raised her concerns about our relationship and how Liam appeared to be controlling me. I'd laughed and told her not to worry; we were in love.

Then, when he'd broken up with me, I'd finally faced how he'd isolated me from my friends, and how much of myself I'd lost to him. Instead of missing him terribly, I'd been relieved to have my life back. It has taken time, but I've slowly built up enough confidence to chase my own dreams, but not confident enough to believe a new romance won't derail them again.

You don't have to be rude, but you should keep Fraser strictly in the friend category.

Lecture over, I pick up my phone from the counter and make my way to the bathroom. When we're at the market tomorrow, I'll make it clear I'm not looking for anything other than friendship. He's not giving out any vibes to make me think that would offend him.

I snuggle into bed and turn on my phone. Declan has sent more family photos from the theme park with a message.

There are two work messages from Liam and one that has I miss you in the preview. I delete them all without reading them. *And this is why I don't need any additional drama in my life.*

There's nothing from Mum or Dad, which is odd. Mum knows I'm unplugging for a month, but I'd let her know I'd be checking for messages. It's unlike her to go more than a couple of days without trying to contact me.

I quickly sneak on to social media to check if Mum's posting anything. There's nothing. They must be having a good time, or is it something else? I shake off the thought. Perhaps they've unplugged for a bit too. Still, I'll send her a message to let her know I'm still alive in case she checks.

I plug my phone in, and turn my Wi-Fi and data roaming off, ready for some picture taking tomorrow. Perhaps I can jolt Mum into some photo action if I share some with her. Then I pick up a new book, and think better of it.

Instead, I turn the Wi-Fi back on and open the ebook app on my phone. A few minutes later I've downloaded the first of Fraser's books—if I'm going to show him mine, I think I should check his out first.

Turning the Wi-Fi back off, I start reading the first Harry Carpenter novel. It's a slow start for me as I don't read a lot of crime fiction. To be honest, this is my first dip into the genre. However, by the second chapter, I'm into the story and I carry on reading until sleep forces me to stop.

Fraser

Sleep is a long time coming. Every time I drop off, I'm haunted by a dimpled smile that leaves me on edge and wanting more. Around four I give up, and make myself a pot of strong coffee—I suspect I'm going to need it.

Out of the kitchen window, I see Kayla's place is dark and quiet. I clearly do not have a similar impact on her ability to switch off.

Curled up on the sofa with a pot of coffee close by, I wade into another first chapter from my course attendees. It's a cosy mystery this time. Not really my thing, but it's a reason-able attempt. As I turn my notes into a report, I second guess my cocky assertion last night that I'm equipped to work on a graphic novel.

I mean, stretching to a cosy mystery is one thing, but a different genre and one that relies on images as much as the story? When I did my degree, we studied different areas of writing, so I'm not starting from scratch, but..., I'm wondering if I let other parts of my body do the thinking last night.

My not being up to the task is one thing. What if Kayla is like my know-it-alls, unable to take constructive criticism? Or, worse still, what if the story is just bad? And why am I so worried about that?

Out the window the world is waking, and I pour myself another cup of coffee. *Why am I making such a big thing of this?* It's not like she's paying me, and she's not a professional writer. By her own admission this is a fun project. All she wants is to make sure she's heading in the right direction, and perhaps get some ideas for improvements.

While I make a bacon butty for breakfast, I do a quick internet search on guidelines for writing a graphic novel. The scene structure for a graphic novel is similar to the way I outline a scene for a book. I can do this.

I can work with that!

Fortified with food and coffee, and my confidence as a writing critic restored, I shower and change, ready to pick Kayla up for the markets.

She's already waiting on the deck, dressed in loose floral cotton trousers and a t-shirt. She grins when she sees me, and I'm mortified when my heart skips a beat as those dimples appear.

"Morning," I say brusquely, hoping to cover my reaction to her.

Slipping a bookmark between the pages of her book, she stands. "I'll just grab my bag."

I wait for her on the deck, hoping she won't be too long —all the best food options will sell out quickly with the holiday crowds around. She returns in a couple of minutes, a large shopping tote and a floppy sun hat in her hand.

"I'm ready," she says, shutting and locking the deck door. "Getting out of bed was hard this morning, so I hope this is as good as you promised."

"It'll be better," I tell her confidently, opening the door to my four-wheel drive. "We get a lot of producers from the Hunter Valley."

Kayla's eyes are wide at the size of my car. "I'll never get up there without help."

Being a tad over six feet, I've never considered how difficult it might be for others to get into my vehicle. When buying it, my chief concern had been whether it would cope with forest tracks when I need a night away in a tent under the stars. I open the door for her, revealing a step and point to the handgrip.

"Ah," she says, then hands me her bag and hat while she clambers in.

When she's settled, I return her possessions. As I reach up to pull the seat belt down for her, I catch a whiff of mango and coconut that draws me in a bit closer than necessary.

"Ah, thank you," she says, shattering the moment.

Feeling awkward, I close the door. Once we're out of the carpark, I feel better, but I'm already thinking about how to avoid another incident this morning. There is definitely something about her I simply can't resist.

"Fraser?"

Her sharp tone pulls me from my thoughts. "Mmm, yeah."

Her hands worry the straps of her bag. This isn't going to be good.

"Just so we're clear, this isn't a date."

"Absolutely not. I don't do holiday romances, not even festive flings." *Anymore.*

Beside me, Kayla's shoulders relax. "Good, we're on the same page then. Just friends."

"Yep, beach buddies." I sound light-hearted, and part of me is relieved to have this clarified. Why then is my stomach sinking as though we've just broken up?

"It's not that I don't find you attractive, or good company," Kayla adds. "But I'm in a transition period after breaking up with my boyfriend and quitting my job. While I'm re-evaluating where I go from here, I don't need any distractions."

So, she thinks I'm attractive and good company. Funny how you focus on what you want to hear. Suddenly, the sick feeling in the pit of my stomach is gone, and a ray of sunshine has brightened my day. *But we're just going to be friends,* I remind myself, and I hope I'm actually listening.

We're some of the first people at the market, so we get a parking spot close by under the shade of some trees. We start with the food stands, and I beam as Kayla "oohs" and "ah's" over the selection. Before hitting the general stalls, we put our purchases in the fridge in the back of the car, which I had thankfully remembered to plug in yesterday in anticipation of a market trip today.

As we wander through the rest of the gazebos, Kayla photographs everything. She asks me to take one of her for her family by the market sign and, as I do, I notice she's got her data turned off.

When I ask about it, she says, "I've spent the last two years working on projects days, nights, weekends, and any time in between. This first month on the beach is for me to rest and rest. I disconnected to let me do that. Next month, when I plan to decide my next steps, I'll need to be back in touch with the world. Until then, it's only messages from family."

She takes her phone back.

"Sounds like bliss," I tell her.

"I think my family enjoys work too much. My dad runs a building company and I think Mum hardly saw him this last year. He's making it up to her by taking her on a cruise this Christmas."

"Lucky mum," I say.

She laughs. "I think she'd really rather have Dad home more. It was talking with her this year that made me realise the impact that living for your work has on others."

I smile. "And you've decided to work to live?"

She laughs again. "Not exactly. It's more that I've decided if I'm going to throw myself into my job, then it'd better be something I love doing."

"And you don't love IT development?"

Her nose wrinkles in a way that's almost as adorable as her dimples. "Not even close. I started out as a graduate doing graphics. When the project manager left for another job, I stepped in and found I was good at getting things done.

Soon I was doing more and more of that, and less and less of the designs. Don't get me wrong, it paid well, and it was my choice. It's just I woke up five years later wondering what I was doing."

"I know that feeling." I tell her.

"That's right. You used to be a journalist."

Now it's my turn to wrinkle my nose. "If you can call it that. I was rewriting stories other people reported and researched, making them internet palatable."

"Writing click bait?" she asks in mock surprise, and I snort.

"I hadn't quite sunk that low, but I was dumbing down stories, making them scannable, which often meant losing substance."

"Then you gave it all up to become an author."

"No, I'm not as brave as you. I'd always written stories and things, but never put them out there. And I didn't give up my job until I had a book deal."

"That must've been exciting!"

It had been until my parents died. They never got to see my first book published.

Kayla places a hand on my arm. "Fraser, what's the matter?"

"I was thinking it sucks that my parents never got to see my first book. They were killed in a car accident while I was still writing it."

"Oh, Fraser, I didn't know. That must have been a nightmare." She squeezes my arm, and I'm surprised by how much I appreciate the sympathy.

I pat her hand before removing my arm. The loss is still

pretty raw almost six years on, and I don't want today to be about that.

"I was struggling to get the book finished, and it was my friends who encouraged me to give up my job and write full time. Well, when I say full time, I also teach, and do the occasional freelance news piece. Gotta scramble to make ends meet when you're an author."

"Would you go back and do things differently, though?"

Considering her circumstances, my answer feels important to her, so I choose my words carefully.

"Some days I would give anything for the security of a regular pay cheque. Other days it's a struggle to get into Harry Carpenter's head and write something I think other people will read. All in all, though, I'm fortunate I get to live where I do, write almost full time, and that people enjoy what I create."

As I speak the words, their truth strikes a note in my heart. Much as I want to work on something I'm more passionate about, I am very lucky to have what I have.

I lead Kayla through the crowd to the coffee van. We arm ourselves with cappuccinos and muffins, then find a table in the surf club's shade.

"You sound excited when you talk about writing," Kayla says. "I want to feel that enthusiastic about what I do."

"What would make you feel that way—the novel you're working on?"

She gnaws on her bottom lip, then twirls her coffee cup on the table.

"Funny, but I don't actually know. As a kid I loved getting lost in drawing, and making up fantasy characters and the worlds they live in. It was a little difficult to think of a career making fantasy characters that didn't involve computer coding, which bored me, so I compromised and studied art and graphic design. That led to my job, which took me even further away from where I want to be. So, at the moment, I'm simply indulging and thinking."

"I caught a sneak peek of your drawings yesterday. I'm no art critic, but they're pretty good."

Kayla's head dips. "Thank you."

"You know there's an artist here who sells his work at other local markets and online. Why not talk to him about how he makes it work?"

Kayla nods, and I'm not sure she's into the idea. Yet, when I introduce her to Ron a few minutes later, they click and I end up strolling around the rest of the markets alone while they talk. When I drag her away an hour or so later, she's invigorated.

"He was so interesting," Kayla says on the drive home. "He has several small income streams from markets, to online sales, to illustrating for authors, and even selling t-shirts."

"Sounds like the life of an artist is like that of an author," I say.

She nods. "And probably for most people in the creative industries. The one big takeaway, though, was that you need to manage your income expectations. If I was to give everything up for my art, I wouldn't be able to carry on living in my flat in Sydney. Not that I'm worried about it for the next year because I've let it, so the mortgage is covered."

"Sounds like you've got a lot to think about," I say, turning into our carpark.

I've barely had time to turn the car off when Barb appears, a golden ball of something wriggling in her arms.

"Did you forget something, Fraser?" she asks as I shut the car door.

CHAPTER 5
OOH, BEACH ROMANCE

Kayla

Fraser turns white. "Oh, Isla's present." His eyes widen in shock. "Is that it? She got me a dog? What was she thinking? I'm off on a signing tour in a month."

Isla? A little worm of jealousy wriggles in my stomach, and I push it down, telling myself I don't care if he's close enough to another woman for her to buy him a dog.

I grab my shopping out of the back of Fraser's car, and by the time I've done that, the puppy is in Fraser's arms, and it's looking up at him with the most adorable liquid brown eyes.

"Don't stress, Fraser," Barb says. "Isla sorted it with me. I'll take care of him when you're away. He's some sort of cocker spaniel cross—the last of a friend of mine's surprise litter. He wanted to get rid of it before Christmas, so Isla got a bargain."

The little ball of fluff is so cute, I can almost see why people get so attached to dogs.

Fraser appears dazed as he cradles the puppy in his arms. "I have nothing at home for..., does he have a name. I've no bed, food.... Is it house trained?"

Barb hands Fraser a piece of paper with writing on it. "He's Peppy, and he's house trained, well, almost, and he's had all of his puppy shots. He came with a crate he's used to sleeping in. On there you'll find food suggestions, there's the vet's number should anything go wrong. His baby teeth haven't come out, so get something for him to chew on while you're out."

Standing there with the pup in his arms and the piece of paper in his hand, Fraser appears incapable of making a decision about anything.

"I'll take your food and put it in my fridge," I say.

Barb takes the pup. "And I'll look after him until you get back."

With Fraser organised, I carry both our purchases down to my cottage and stow the food. Inspired by my conversation with Ron, I feel excited about painting for the first time in..., I can't remember when.

I set up a piece of watercolour paper on the easel and sketch out my main female character, the young trainee spy, paying special attention to her clothing to make sure she has enough pockets for the variety of knives she carries. On another sheet, I do the same for my new male character, the Captain of the Guard. Half-way through I change my mind, and start again, aging down my male spy to late teens, and merging him with the guard captain character I drew of Fraser yesterday.

When I'm happy with their outlines, I set out my paints,

brushes and bits and pieces, and fill a couple of jars with clean water. Before I start, I change into a pair of cut-off jeans and an old t-shirt. Then I'm ready.

I spend the afternoon working on one portrait, then the other, while I wait for the last bit of work to dry. I'm so engrossed in what I'm doing, I don't notice the time passing until a scrabbling at the door draws me from my fantasy world. Looking up, I find Fraser framed by the door, his new housemate sitting at his feet, patting at the glass.

When he sees he has my attention, Fraser slides the door open before bending, picking up the pup and stepping inside in a single fluid movement. "Is it a good time to collect my food?"

I nod. "Sure, come in."

"And I want to invite you to dinner this evening as a thank you for helping me out."

As I move past Fraser to get the bag of food, Fraser places the pup on the floor and he jumps for me. I take a step back; I've never really felt comfortable around dogs.

Fraser picks up the puppy and stares into his eyes as he says in a low voice, "Peppy, no." The dog drops his head. "Sorry, puppies can be impulsive until they're fully trained."

"You've had dogs before?" I ask, attempting to cover my embarrassment at being scared by the tiny bundle of fur.

Fraser scratches the dog behind his ear. "We always had dogs at home. Isla, my sister, took my parents' dog in when they died. She always felt bad about it, especially as I live on my own. This must be her way of making up for it."

I hand him the bag of food and tentatively pat the dog's head. His fur is smooth, almost like silk. His small pink tongue flicks out and he licks my hand. I resist the urge to pull away, and am rewarded by the dog resting his head on my fingers, trapping me.

As I smile at the pup, I'm suddenly aware of the warm, musky smell of Fraser, and the heat of his body. I glance up and find his dark chocolate eyes watching me, a smile playing around the corner of his mouth. My eyes drift to those lips, and for a moment..., I jerk away and Peppy whimpers.

"I'd love to come for dinner. What time?"

"Now, if that suits."

I glance out the window, surprised to find the sky darkening over the water. "I'll have to tidy up here and get changed."

"What you're wearing's fine. Hold on, is that me?"

"What?"

He moves over to my easel, which is displaying my main character, who is now a teenage version of Fraser. Heat rushes to my face. Of course, that would have to be the picture I was working on when he turned up, not my blue-haired heroine.

"I did sort of base him on you. I hope you don't mind."

His face splits into a huge grin. "You've turned me into a fantasy hero—I'm flattered. Do I have any superpowers?"

"Not superpowers, exactly. But you can hide in shadows and blend into things so people don't know you're there."

"Cool. And am I a prince?"

I shake my head. "You're a spy."

He cocks his head to the side, and Peppy mirrors his

actions as if he's also considering my painting too. For a moment I wonder if Fraser's going to be offended.

"I think I like that better. And the painting, it's pretty cool."

He nods as if confirming this to himself, then turns for the door. "Dinner's only going to be a simple pasta, so don't take too long," he says as he leaves.

I watch him go, a tumult of emotions washing through me. There is no way Fraser can have looked at the details in the painting and not realised I've been watching him. Now I'm going to have dinner with him. What am I doing? I can't back out now.

Cleaning my brushes and tidying my paints allows me to concentrate on something other than Fraser MacIntosh. So, by the time I close the deck door behind me, I'm certain I'm back in friend mode and able to face dinner alone with my hero neighbour who spends so much time in my imagination.

Fraser

Peppy sniffs around the deck enclosure I've made for him while I prep dinner. He chomps on the chew toy I bought, then drops from exhaustion on the bed inside his crate. By the time Kayla arrives carrying a bottle of wine, he's completely out for the count.

Kayla's wine is a local white from the Hunter Valley, and I

nod approvingly. It's crisp and fresh, and will go perfectly with the seafood pasta I'm making. As she hands it over, I can't help but notice the paint around the fingernails of her right hand. She grimaces when she notices what I'm looking at.

"Sorry, a downside of painting. I didn't have time to do a full scrub."

"No worries," I say. "Wine glasses are in there. Do you want to pour us a drink?"

As she hands me a glass of wine, she asks if there's anything else she can do.

"No, I've got it all under control." Dropping the fresh linguine into the pot of boiling water, I gesture to the deck. "Sit down and enjoy the view. I'll bring the food out in a minute."

A few minutes later, I take the seat at the end of the table so I can see her and the view.

"Goodness, a superhero and a chef," she says, bending her head and savouring the aroma of the bowl of pasta in front of her. In the flickering candlelight, I watch her as she takes her first mouthful. "This is amazing."

I grin, more than happy she appreciates my cooking. "It's one of my mum's family recipes."

"Your mum was Italian?"

"She was."

"But how did you get such a Scottish name?"

She clearly hasn't read my online bio, and it's refreshing not to have had someone look me up on the internet. "Mum is second generation Australian. Her dad came over at the end of World War Two. My dad, on the other hand, was born in Glasgow and came to Aus on an overseas trip. He met Mum and never left."

I wait for her to react the way most people do when they hear how my parents met. A wicked glint sparkles in her eyes. "I'm pleased you take after your mother. I don't think I would've been able to turn you into a spy if you had flaming red hair. You'd stand out way too much."

I bark out a laugh, startling Peppy. "I'm gutted that you think so little of my heritage," I say, overdoing the mock hurt in my voice.

Actually, I'm not gutted at all. Normally when I tell people about my parents, they gush at how romantic their story is, and how tragic it was that they died so young. But that wasn't all my parents were about. They loved each other deeply, but family was as important to them as they were to each other. They were more than the sum of how they met.

Kayla's hand slips over the top of mine. "You miss them a lot, don't you?"

I nod. "I feel a bit, I don't know, unanchored without them."

"How come you're not spending Christmas with your sister?" she asks, removing her hand.

The question seems to come out of left field, but I get where she's coming from.

"I *would* normally spend Christmas with her and her family, but this year I..., I don't know, I let work get in the way."

"Is this about the TV deal you mentioned?"

I fiddle with the stem of the wineglass. "Yes, and no."

"It must be exciting having your books picked up for TV."

I stare at my wine, wondering how best to answer that. "At first it was. Then I spoke to other authors, and the first thing you realise is that, once you've sold the rights, you lose control. Which means I won't be a part of bringing the books to life for viewers. Once you get over that, then it becomes more about money. More about how much are you prepared to sell your idea for."

"Oh, I didn't realise. Is that bad?"

"Gosh, I must sound like a sad sack. If it happens, it will be cool to see Harry Carpenter in the flesh, and I'm not sneezing at the money. It'll buy opportunities for me. I guess the only downside is that I had thought it would buy me time to try something new. Instead, it looks like it will tie me into writing more Harry Carpenter books for the foreseeable future."

I can't believe I'm opening up to Kayla like this. Normally, I'm a lot more guarded about my work life, and my feelings come to think of it. Maybe it's the good food and wine, or the fact I'm relaxed after finishing my book. Mostly, though, I think it's because she's bewitched me with those soft green eyes.

"And that's bad because...?" she prompts, and I find myself answering.

"It gets a little stale writing about the same characters. I'm ready for a new project."

"Can't you do both?"

I laugh, and it's a pretty self-depreciating sound. "Look at me taking up the entire conversation with my sad tale of the poor boy who got everything he wants and still finds something to complain about."

Kayla's head tilts to the side, like she's trying to work something out about me. Just when I'm feeling the urge to fill the void, she speaks.

"It would have been so easy for you to rest on your laurels, to write Harry Carpenter books for ever and ever. It says something about you that you want to try new things."

I can't hold her gaze. I'm a fraud. She has no idea how risk adverse I am.

Gathering the plates, I push myself to my feet. "Coffee?"

"Please."

In the privacy of the kitchen, I centre myself and make a promise to change the subject from me when I return.

Carrying the coffee back onto the deck, I'm startled to find Peppy curled up on Kayla's lap. She'd given the impression she wasn't comfortable around dogs, yet here she is gently stroking the little guy.

Peppy raises his head as I put the drinks on the table, and I swear the look he's giving me says, "She's mine. Don't even think about moving me."

The look I send in return has a definite "We'll see about that" vibe.

Then I shake my head. I can't believe I'm getting into head games with a dog over a woman I'm only friends with.

"Seems like Peppy's made himself at home," I say.

"I hope it's okay. He came over and looked up at me with those enormous eyes. I haven't spent much time with dogs, so I didn't know."

"It's fine. I can see he's going to be trouble though, wrapping everyone round his finger."

She grins. "A babe magnet, you might say."

We laugh as the puppy settles back down and we fall into a companionable silence. All too soon, Peppy breaks the mood by stirring and searching for a way to get down. Kayla places him back on the ground, and I open the makeshift gate I set up and take him down off the deck. Kayla follows.

"It's getting late. I should be going." She holds up her hand when I object. "I'd love to stay longer, but I'm beat after an early morning and a mammoth painting session."

"Okay," I say, not even trying to hide my disappointment.

"Thanks so much for the meal. Perhaps I can return the favour tomorrow night—although don't expect anything as gourmet as your dinner."

Peppy nudges my leg and I pick him up in one hand. Then, without thinking it through, I lean down and kiss her cheek. I catch a waft of tropical mango and resist the urge to close my eyes and drink the smell of her in. Instead, I say in the most casual tone I can muster, "See you tomorrow."

For a moment Kayla freezes in place and I wonder if I've overstepped. Then she comes to life, turns and takes a couple of steps down the path before half-turning back.

"Six-thirtyish." Is it my imagination, or is her voice a little strained?

Watching her walk away, I reconcile myself to another restless night with dreams of dark-red hair, green eyes, dimples, and delightful curves. Keeping my distance from the alluring Kayla is getting harder and harder, and I'm wondering if it's what I really want anymore.

Kayla

I toss and turn, unable to fall asleep as I keep replaying Fraser's kiss, and that moment after when I had to stop myself from reaching up and lacing my fingers through his hair before pulling him in closer so I could feel those soft lips against mine.

At some stage I must have slept. When I wake, it's with the memory of Fraser's lips on my cheek. Tracing my fingers over the spot where he kissed me, I berate myself for my reaction to something so chaste.

"No," I groan. "I don't need this! I have to keep my distance. No more kisses, we're just friends."

In search of a distraction, I reach over and pick up my phone. Turning on the data, I wait a moment for the messages to ping before scrolling through.

The first is from Declan, who's responded to the pics I sent through yesterday with some of his own. Still nothing from Mum, even though I sent her through some photos too. Guess I'll have to send her something a little more exciting to tempt her away from her cruise fun.

I delete the messages from Liam, not even bothering to check the content, then turn my phone off and head out for a walk along the beach to clear my head and plan my day. The sea air is refreshing this early in the morning, and I enjoy the solitude and time to think.

When I get back, I shower and have a quick breakfast before checking the fridge. At the markets yesterday, I'd had a favourite dish in mind to make, though I hadn't intended to make it for Fraser. Sitting front and centre is the round of pork from the butcher, and from the cupboard I retrieve the mixed peppercorns and rock salt I'd bought from a spice merchant. I prep the pork, ready to put on this afternoon, cover it, and pop it back in the fridge.

While the door is open, I make sure I have everything I need to make the rocket, macadamia and mango salad that goes with it, then put the food from my mind.

Today is about starting to properly storyboard my novel. After Fraser opened up to me last night, I've decided I trust him enough with my project to ask for his input. I'm keen to give him the outline and a couple of storyboards so he gets an idea of my vision.

Only stopping briefly to make a sandwich for lunch, I work through the day, caught up in the world I'm creating. When the alarm goes off at four, I heat the barbecue. When it's at temperature, I put the pork on, close the lid, then get pulled back into my story.

I'm feeling proud of how everything is going to plan until I hear the patter of paws on the wood of the deck. Dammit, the pork!

"Hi," I say to Fraser as I rush past him to open the barbecue cover and jab a fork in the roast. Juice still runs out. Phew, I might have saved it.

I remove the pan from the flames and carry it carefully inside. As I take the pork out and cover it to rest, I notice Fraser hovering by my easel, Peppy tucked under his arm to keep him out of mischief. My head screams at me to whip the work in progress away, but I over-rule it and ask Fraser what he'd like to drink.

"I've brought some beers," he says, pointing to a cooler bag on the bench.

There are half a dozen bottles from a local brewery inside. I put four into the fridge and pour the remaining two into glasses. Taking the drinks over to Fraser, I hand him one.

"Do you mind if I have a look?" He gestures to my storyboards with his bottle.

I'm still not comfortable with him looking at my work, but I do want his opinion. Time to take the plunge. "No, but please be gentle."

I keep quiet while he reads, my heart in my mouth as he turns each page. When he places the original storyboard back, I pick up the notebook with the story and chapter outlines and say, "Those are just for the opening chapter. The full story is in here." I hold the book out.

Fraser gives a sexy eyebrow raise and asks, "You trust me with your book?"

I almost chicken out. Then I suck in a breath and force out a "Yes."

He looks at the book, his beer, and then at Peppy, and I laugh. "Come outside and sit down. You don't have to read this now, but I still have the salad to make, so it might fill in the time."

As I pull together the meal, I can't help but sneak a quick glance outside to see if Fraser is actually reading my novel— he is. My stomach flips and I feel a little ill. Closing my eyes, I take a calming breath. *What's the worst that could happen? OMG, what if he hates it?*

I gulp in air and concentrate on putting the salad together, telling myself that it's better to know if it's horrendous now, rather than in three weeks' time when I've put my whole holiday into it. When I take the food out, Peppy is asleep on the chair beside Fraser, and he is staring out at the ocean.

"Would you like another beer?" I ask when I notice his glass is empty.

"Thanks." He smiles up at me. "That one went down way too fast."

I bring him out another bottle before sitting opposite him. He pours his beer as I start on my dinner.

"Sorry we're eating off our laps," I say. "My work's taken over the only table in the place."

He grins at me. "I guess that's the problem with holiday lets. They don't always have everything you need."

Put me out of my misery, tell me what you think of my book, I scream in my head as I take a mouthful of pork. It's a little less juicy than I'd like, but it still tastes good.

"Mmm, this is nice," Fraser says, as he cuts another piece of meat.

I can't stand it any longer, and I blurt out, "What did you think?" I nod to my outline sitting on the coffee table between us. "Be honest. I can take it. It's not as deep as yours...." I run out of words.

"I got the impression you hadn't read any of my books," Fraser says, taking a swig of his beer.

"I had to check you out before I trusted you with my baby."

He laughs, and somehow that makes me feel a little less tense.

"Well..., it's a different genre," Fraser starts, and I immediately tense for the blow.

"True," I say, attempting to keep the frustration from my voice.

"But the principles of telling a story and keeping a reader hooked are the same. Your story idea is sound, but on a first read through, you need a bit more tension to keep the reader hooked."

"Tension?"

"Yep. An easy way to do that is by incorporating failures into the story, or heightening a risk."

I think I get what he's saying, but I must look confused, because he says, "Let me give you an example. When your guys are trying to get into the palace, why not make their only point of entry three stories up? Then you could have them enter an occupied room and almost get caught. Or, perhaps when they're trying to get to the study, they could run into a guard."

"Ah, I think I get it. I could make it even more chaotic. Like they enter a bathroom where someone is having a bath. The person screams and the guard arrives."

His grin is genuine and I'm really excited now. I can see some other areas where I could make similar changes. Okay, I might have to alter an outline or two, but that should be okay.

"You want to make those changes now, don't you?" Fraser says.

"How did you—"

"I'm a writer too."

A writer too. That comment sends heat to my cheeks. So my story isn't that bad.

"I do want to work on it now, but I'm also enjoying a meal with you. The story will still be there tomorrow."

Beside Fraser, Peppy snuffles as if in agreement, and we both laugh.

For the rest of the meal, we put novels and stories aside and find we have heaps to talk about. We drift from topic to topic, finding we have more in common than strong family connections like we both secretly enjoy country music and hate lying about in bed.

As we exchange ideas, we also find we disagree on a range of things from the solutions to climate change and whether living off-grid is sustainable to whether the original Dr Who is better than the reboots. These discussions only make the evening more interesting.

Fraser has seconds, and we both have another beer. Peppy barks to be taken off the deck, and that's my cue to make coffee. I serve it with some handmade chocolates I bought yesterday.

"How did you know I'm a sucker for chocolates?" Fraser asks as he steps back onto the deck and reaches out to help me with the tray.

"Think of it as a thank you for looking at my novel."

His eyes twinkle as he says, "My rates are normally steeper than that."

"Oh yeah." I tease, feeling a little giddy and reckless. Those beers must be strong. "What would I normally have to pay?"

His eyes darken and are filled with such longing that all

my good intentions about staying friends drift from my mind.

Don't do it, Kayla—it'll only end in tears.

My mind tries a last-ditch attempt to call for sanity, but it's already too late. I'm leaning in, overcome by his closeness, and the kiss I imagined last night is nowhere near as meltingly sweet as the one we share tonight.

Then, all too soon, it's over.

"We, ah, seem to have abandoned the friend thing," he says, his voice husky and his face flushed.

I send him a slow smile. "Let's think of it as a business transaction, and I'll consider my debt paid in full."

While I try to keep my tone light, my alter-ego tells me this is more than a thank you, and it wants more..., much more than that one kiss.

We can't find that easy camaraderie again while we drink our coffee and, all too soon, Fraser rises to leave.

"Sorry, I've got an early start tomorrow. I have a meeting in Sydney with my agent. If you want to make some changes to your outlines and drop it by mine, I'll have a look at it on Tuesday."

I walk Fraser down the steps, my good angel tells me to keep it chill. The devil on my other shoulder urges me to be bold and take another chance. "Kiss him again," it urges. I watch him fade into the darkness, feeling more than a little confused and frustrated.

Fraser

That kiss last night is all I can think about as I drive down to Sydney. I should go over options for the meeting with Phil, my agent, but every time I try to focus on work, my mind replays that kiss again. The feel of her lips as they moved beneath mine, and what it did to every fibre of my being.

No doubt, if I let myself go, I could fall for Kayla, but the timing and everything else is crap. I have to concentrate on the future, and I'll be heading away on a book tour soon, and she has so much going on in her life. As I park the car outside the restaurant, I give myself a stern talking too. *It was nothing. It won't happen again. Let it go.*

Phil is already waiting when I enter, and I can tell from the serious look on his face I'm not going to like what he has to tell me. At least he's considerate enough to wait until we're finished with our starters.

"Now we've done the pleasantries, I guess we should do the business so I can expense this." He laughs a little nervously, but I don't feel the need to help him out here. I have too much riding on this conversation. "Fraser, historic fiction just doesn't sell as well, and you'd be competing for market share against some really big names."

"So, they said they're not interested."

"They did. But I have the contract here for the Harry Carpenter books, and the advance isn't to be sneezed at."

Five books over five years. That won't give me time for much else, what with promotions and teaching. Is this what I want? It will certainly go a long way towards securing the TV contract, and that will buy me some space later on.

My mind goes blank. Now I wish I'd done some more thinking in the car. At the very least, I should have gone over some options for Phil to take back. Phil pulls a pen from his pocket and offers it to me.

"I've been through the details and it's a pretty good offer, especially given the state of the industry."

I turn to the schedule at the back outlining payments and delivery schedules. From what I understand, after talking with other authors, Phil has done pretty well for me. Still, I don't take the pen. It's now or never. I push the contract back across the table.

"How about this? I'd accept a reduced advance if we change the contract to five books over six years."

Phil's jaw drops. I've never questioned his advice. He's the one who steered me down this track in the first place, he's the first person who believed my work was more than just bedroom scribbles.

"This is about you writing your historic fiction, isn't it?" he asks.

I nod. "I want a chance to write it, Phil."

"How much do you want it?"

I shake my head. "I don't get what you're asking."

He runs a hand through his greying hair. "I mean, Fraser, would you blow this deal for it?"

Would I? I don't know.

"Just ask, Phil. If you don't ask, you don't get."

"It won't sell like these books do," Phil says.

"I know."

"And it might hurt your brand."

"Isn't that what pen names are for?" I ask.

He laughs. "Okay. I guess we all have a project in us we have to do. Let me ask the question and get back to you."

With business out of the way, the rest of the meal is relaxed. We talk about Christmas plans, and family, and the state of the publishing industry in general. When I leave the restaurant, I'm pretty relaxed, even though my future income is still up in the air. As I walk along the street, my stomach knots. *What am I doing trading financial security for a dream?* This is so unlike me. Perhaps Kayla is having more than a physical impact on me. Her adventurous spirit might be inspiring me to dare a little.

Speaking of Kayla, I head into my favourite bookshop and browse the graphic novel section. I can't say it's something I've ever done before, and I'm surprised at the range of novels available. There are even some graphic novel versions of the classics. I grab a couple of classics, including a Jane Austen, which is so not my style, to see how they've been handled, and a couple of fantasy ones too.

The drive home couldn't have been more different from the drive down. When I stop to fill up for gas, I almost call Phil to tell him I'm on my way back to sign the contract. It's only the poor cell reception that prevents me.

When I stop into Barb's to pick up Peppy, I'm relieved when she offers me a drink. I've been alone with my own thoughts for too long today, and I need some perspective. I tell Barb about my meeting and she listens without commenting.

"So, no sage advice?" I finally ask.

"Perhaps Kayla's life experience is rubbing off on you."

Her flip response annoys me, and I don't quite know

why. "Barb, I've been thinking about writing this book for years."

"Don't get your knickers in a twist. All I'm saying is that seeing someone else follow their dreams often makes us question our own paths."

Feeling a little contrite, I offer a heartfelt, "Sorry. I guess I'm a little tense."

"Humph. You two have been spending a bit of time together the last couple of days."

"We're not sleeping together, if that's what you're asking," I snap.

"Calm the farm, Fraser."

It's like Barb is pushing all my buttons tonight, and I don't know why.

"Look, this is not about you doing the holiday thing and getting your heart broken again. This is a little deeper than that."

I scrub a hand over my face. I'm too tired to guess at what she's getting at. "Just say what you mean, Barb."

"I think you're both at turning points in your lives, and you're clearly attracted to one another. All I'm saying is, be careful, and make sure you're making decisions for you and not because you think you're being challenged."

"I am inspired by her taking a leap and giving up her job, no doubt. But you know me, Barb. I won't make a hasty decision, and I won't wreck my career over a story I want to write."

"And what about Kayla?"

"I'm just offering her some advice. From what I saw in

the bookshop today, her idea has potential. I'd love to see her finish it."

"And no romance?"

"Even if I was prepared to break my rule and embark on a festive fling, she's made it clear she is only looking for friendship."

"She's a lovely girl, Fraser, and I had hoped you could help her by offering her some writing advice. As to the romance side though, I get the sense there's some unfinished business there, Fraser, and I wouldn't like you to get caught in the middle."

My talk to myself clearly had no effect, as my heart sinks when Barb alludes to another love interest. Kayla had briefly mentioned a break up, but I hadn't wanted to delve into that, and so had skipped it. I'm still not ready to deal with it, so I stand and pick up Peppy.

"I'd better get Peppy home. We've got a big few days coming up and we both need our sleep."

Despite her initial calming influence, I leave Barb's place feeling more unsettled than when I arrived. There's a notebook on the outdoor table when I get home—Kayla's revisions. I put Peppy to bed, but I'm still too wired after the drive to sleep. Flicking through Kayla's work, I toy with the idea of reading it now. I put it back down because I want to study the books I bought today before I critique her story again.

Wandering into my office, I look for something to distract myself. I decide to search for the story pitch and original research I did for my novel. When my laptop has booted, I scan the files and eventually find the folder in my archives.

Reading the documents through is a revelation, and I don't know what to think. Five books later, I find the work amateur. The story line about the murder of a convict woman on a boat from England to Australia still appeals. The original idea was to have the captain put it down to acceptable losses, but a young woman convict convinces a junior adjutant on board to investigate it as murder. What had drawn me to this type of murder mystery was the rawness of the environment and the basic investigative tools my main characters would have used to solve the mystery. Okay, researching the history also appeals.

Pulling up a new document, I type and I don't stop for some time. I roll into bed around five, having outlined the first section of the book and taken notes for the research I'll need to do.

Kayla

It's lunchtime and I still haven't heard from Fraser. *And there's no reason why I should have,* I remind myself for the umpteenth time. *He has his own work to be getting on with.*

Yesterday, I went online to research creating tension in storytelling before sitting down and working on my rewrite. Although I keep telling myself Fraser probably won't even get to my story today, I worry I've been too clever and made the story worse. The devil on my shoulder keeps telling me Fraser hates it, and now he's avoiding me so he doesn't have to admit I've made a hash of it.

What do I care! Defiantly, I grab my keys and make my way to the carpark.

I *do* care. Last night, I finished his book, and surprisingly, I enjoyed it. He's a talented writer. He drew me in and made me care about the characters in his story.

And, I have to admit, I kinda like him. He's becoming a good friend, and I enjoy his company. I don't want to lose that friendship over something as inconsequential as my scribblings. The devil on my shoulder smirks. *Just friends? You're delusional.*

"Argh, this waiting around is torture!"

Christmas is only a few days away, and there is nothing Christmasy in my house. While I'm out, I'll grab some food for the get together tomorrow night at Barb's.

When I return from town, I can see through the window above the TV that Fraser is home too. *No, I won't think about him.* I put up my ready decorated, artsy wooden Christmas tree, and place the Christmas gnomes around the base. I then get my presents from my family out of the case under the bed and place them on the floor.

The pile is small compared to other years, a reminder of how isolated I became from my friends while I was with Liam. That's why connecting with my true self is essential, as it may allow me to reconnect with them.

Fraser still hasn't appeared, so I change into painting clothes, having decided on the way home to work on some cover art to distract myself.

As the sun goes down, the light fades, and I have to stop. While I cook myself some fried rice for dinner, I check my phone. Still nothing from Mum. For a moment I consider messaging Dad, but he never responds to texts. Perhaps I'll give it another day, then try calling.

I scroll through the family snaps Declan sent and delete some more messages from Liam. There's a knock at the door as I'm turning the data back off.

It's Fraser and Peppy, who's on a leash today because Fraser has an armload of books, with a printout of something and my outline notebook perched precariously on top. As I open the door, Peppy rushes forward and Fraser's pile topples.

While Fraser gathers the printed pages and tries to order them, I bend to pick up his books, and I'm surprised to find they're a collection of graphic novels. Peppy slides under my hand, demanding a pat as I say, "What are these for?"

"I had to do some research because I wanted to make sure I got this right for you."

My heart warms at the care he's putting into my project. "I thought fantasy isn't your thing," I say to cover the intensity of what I'm feeling.

"That's why I got a couple of classics too." He points to the two books left on the floor. "One of them is a romance, just in case I need to bone up on that as well."

I grab the last two books before standing.

"Umm, your food...," Fraser says, and I shove the books at him.

Making my way to the kitchen, I trip over Peppy's lead and stop myself from falling by grabbing the bench. My visitors have me feeling all at sixes and sevens, but I manage to rescue most of the rice. Only a little of it had stuck to the bottom of the pan.

"Do you want to join me for dinner?" I ask.

Fraser laughs, and I say defensively, "It's not burnt. And I can cook up some salmon to go with it."

"Okay. Thank you. While you do that, let me get this stuff ordered, and sort Peppy out. I think you've been enough trouble tonight," he says to the dog, who looks up with a woeful expression that has me wanting to pick him up and cuddle him.

By the time I've recovered the fried rice and cooked the salmon, Fraser and Peppy have made themselves at home on the deck. I place the tray with the food, a pitcher of iced tea, and some glasses on the table. After pouring us both a tea, I get a bowl with some water for Peppy, before sitting across from Fraser.

"So," I start, "what took you so long today?"

Fraser has a couple of mouthfuls of his dinner before responding. "For someone who didn't want my help, you're rather eager."

I snort. Is he teasing me? "It felt like torture waiting all day for you to come back to me. I kept imagining all the bad things you'd say."

Fraser smiles ruefully. "Sorry, it can be quite nerve-wracking waiting for editors to get back to you, and it doesn't get any easier, believe me."

He places his plate on the table half-eaten and reaches for my notebook.

"I got involved doing some writing last night and wanted

to catch a couple of hours' sleep before getting into your work."

Guilt wells up inside me. Of course, he had his own projects to finish. It was only my anxiety telling me his silence meant he hated my story. "Fraser, you shouldn't have worried about my stuff. Writing is your living."

He grins. "This wasn't for a commissioned book. Anyway, I had to read a couple of graphic novels so I could get a feel for how they work. Then I reviewed what you'd done."

He hands me the notebooks and, as I put my plate on the table, he picks his dinner up and continues eating while I read his notes. There are a lot of them, and my stomach sinks.

"Don't look so worried. The story is way better, but I realised that it would have been much easier to review this if I had the storyboards. Most of my notes are questions about what the images will contribute."

I read through the first couple of pages and I can't help the grin spreading across my face. His comments are a mixture of suggestions and smiley faces, and there are only a few cross outs. Pulling my eyes away from his words, I beam at him.

"Thank you for doing this."

"It was my pleasure, and I'm surprised by how much I actually enjoyed it. Even with my limited experience, I can see you have something pretty cool there. Actually, I have to admit I was initially a bit snobby about fantasy writing, but you have converted me. I can't wait to see the finished product."

As I eat the rest of my dinner, I'm sure I'm glowing. I'm so wrapped up in my happiness I take a minute to remember that Fraser brought over some loose papers. They appear to have disappeared in amongst the books. I'm intrigued by them, but I'm not sure we're good enough friends for me to ask about them outright. *Dang it, they might be important.*

"Fraser, what were the papers on the floor? Were they more notes for my book?"

My dinner guest smiles shyly. "No, they're what I was working on last night. I'd thought I was ready to share them, but I'm not."

Disappointment and curiosity war within me. "Is this something new?" I prompt.

Fraser moves some food around his plate, and I get the impression he's trying to decide whether or not to share with me.

"I'm a good listener, and I can keep things to myself."

Finally, he glances up, takes a breath, and tells me about the book he's been wanting to write for years.

"I'm excited about it, but it will take a lot of time to write and research. And time is something I won't have if I sign the new deal with my publishers," he finishes up.

I want to tell him his story sounds amazing and to go for it—to tell him that following your dreams is important. Then I remember how hard it was for me to walk away from my job and having an income. I also remember how gutting it was letting out the flat I had saved so hard to get the deposit for because I didn't know how long I'd be able to pay the mortgage without work. No doubt it will be equally gutting to move back in with my parents if I can't find a job in the New Year. My savings won't last forever after all.

Fraser's project sounds big, and to finish it will take time away from the things he does to make money. While I'm on a break from the world, beach Kayla wants others to follow their dreams like me. Fortunately, the real world Kayla is still in there, and when she speaks she says, "Fraser, your book idea sounds amazing. I hope when you're feeling up to it, you'll share some of it with me. I also hope you eke out some time to write it."

Perhaps this is being more than a friend, and the butterflies in my stomach flutter as I wonder if I've pushed too hard. When Fraser's lips form a sweet, shy smile, the butterflies fairly dance. "I think I'd like that too."

Times stops, as if we're on the precipice of something. I lean forward in my seat in anticipation. Then, Peppy snuffles, stands up, stares at Fraser, yips, and then the moment is gone.

Fraser holds my gaze, and Peppy yips again. Releasing an enormous sigh, Fraser stands and grabs the pup's lead. "Come on, then." He takes the dog off the deck and over to the bushes.

Feeling a little shaky after the intensity of the last couple of minutes, I clear the plates onto the tray and take them into the kitchen. When I return, Peppy is rushing back onto the deck, Fraser in his wake. Tripping over the dog's trailing lead, I nearly bowl Fraser over as I try to recover my balance. His powerful arms wrap around me to save me from toppling, and before I have time to think, his lips are on mine and I'm lost in his kiss.

Fraser

The sound of claws on wood wakes me. I've only had Peppy a couple of days and he's already got me well trained. I force open an eye and take a moment to adjust to the strange room that is somehow familiar. After last year I had thought I would never set foot in this room again, swore I wouldn't do this again, but somehow with Kayla this feels…, right.

Beside me, the bed moves as a warm body snuggles closer into my side. Memories of last night rush back into my head, bringing a smile to my face, and sending a warmth through my body that starts low in my belly. I want to wrap myself around Kayla and luxuriate in the feel of her against me. The only thing stopping me is the continued scratching and the high-pitched yips of an impatient pup .

I blow out a sigh and roll out of bed. While I pull on my boxer shorts, Peppy scampers to the back door, and is waiting not so patiently when I arrive. I open the door and close it gently behind me as I let Peppy out for his morning snuffle and pee.

He's excited by the unfamiliar scents in the small back-yard, and I let him have a good sniff around. Leaning against the wall, I hear car wheels grind over gravel in the car park. Who is moving about this early in the morning? It can't even be seven yet.

A car door slams, and it is followed by two voices, one I recognise as Barb's. Someone arriving then. It must be Sam and Justine, although this is really early for them.

"Hey, buddy, we're going to meet some new friends today," I tell Peppy, but he ignores me. "Well, I'm excited to be catching up with old friends, even if you're not."

The sound of crunching gravel draws closer, followed by a door knock close by. Someone is at Kayla's door. I tuck Peppy under my arm, slip through the side gate, and sneak a peek round the corner. I'm in time to see a drowsy Kayla open the sliding door. Then there is a flicker of recognition, and what might be a flicker of displeasure. "Liam, what are you doing here?" Her voice rises in surprise.

"You haven't answered your phone, or any of the texts I sent. I was getting worried, and I missed you."

There is silence, then Kayla says, "Liam, you can't just turn up out of the blue like th—"

"I tried to ring last night. Then I texted."

"But I didn't invite you." Kayla's voice is weary, and becoming a touch combative.

"I've driven a long way. The least you can do is invite me

in." The man steps forward, pressing Kayla to move out of the way.

Again there is a pause as Kayla looks over her shoulder, perhaps looking for Peppy and me, then draws her bottom lip between her teeth.

Every fibre of my being wants to join her on the deck, to stand by her side and face whatever this is together. It's not only that I'm hardly appropriately dressed to receive visitors that holds me back, it's also because I'm not one hundred percent sure I'd be welcome.

My worries are confirmed as Kayla's guest takes another step forward, and she moves to let him in. "Um, yes, I guess so. I could put on some coffee."

Kayla follows the man, who is probably her ex-boyfriend, inside. I stand there, frozen, unsure what to do. After last night I had thought..., had hoped.... "Bugger," I say under my breath. Barb warned me about not getting involved because Kayla was getting over someone.

Everything happened so quickly last night I didn't get a chance to ask where things stand with her ex. Is there a possibility she might get back with him? I'm torn between wanting to go inside and rescue Kayla from an uncomfortable situation, or waiting for her to tell me what she needs from me. I could simply return via the back door and saunter in as if I didn't know she had a guest. Dammit, if only we'd exchanged phone numbers I'd be able to at least text her and find out what she wants.

"Come on, Peppy, breakfast," I whisper as I make my way back along the path. I've almost made it home without incident when I turn the corner and find the Frawley children camped out on my deck.

I freeze. Should I duck back into the bushes? Will they even notice?

"Why are you in your undies?" the youngest asks.

"Ellie!" The oldest shushes her, mortification showing on her face—although I can guarantee she's not nearly as mortified as I am.

"I um, Peppy needed to go out," I say. It's not a lie, as such.

"Can we play with Peppy?" the boy asks.

"He's a bit small to play with yet. You can pet him for a bit while I get his breakfast," I say.

Peppy sits up on a cushion and allows the kids to pat him while I nip inside, pull on some shorts, and return with a bowl of kibble.

"Let him eat," the older girl tells the others, and they fall back to watch Peppy devour his food.

Scoffing down his kibble in a matter of seconds, the cheeky wretch, he turns begging eyes on the children.

"He's still hungry," the youngest girl complains.

"No, he's not," I tell them. "He's just trying it on."

The boy stands up. "Come on, this is boring. Let's get Mum and Dad up."

The youngest girl stays put until the other two grab her hands and pull her along.

"Thanks," the oldest girl throws over her shoulder before they disappear from view.

"Well, Peppy, this has been an interesting start to the day," I say.

The pup looks up at me and yawns. I bring out his crate and water bowl, and place them beside the puppy pee pad in his deck enclosure. Putting him inside the crate, I wait until he curls up, ready to sleep, before making sure there's no way for him to get out.

"I need a run," I tell him, though I needn't have bothered because he's asleep before I finish the sentence.

As I follow the track around the edge of the sand, I tell myself I won't check out what's happening at Kayla's place, but I can't resist a peek. She's sitting outside, snuggled in a dressing gown, drinking coffee with the sandy-haired Liam who turned up this morning. The guy's chatting away, punctuating his words with hand gestures every few seconds. Kayla is more subdued. Dare I hope that she's not that pleased he turned up?

I shake off the thought. Great though it was, last night was spur of the moment. I can't relive last year..., I won't relive last year. If Kayla wants us to be more than a one-night stand, then I need her to give me a sign. And I have better things to spend my time worrying over than sexy redheads who've wormed their way under my skin.

"Timing, hey?" I say to no one in particular.

When I hit the sand, I stop and stretch before making my way to the edge of the water where the receding tide has left a hard surface for me to run along. I allow myself a quick glance at Kayla's place before I run. Determined to get her out of my head I start out at a sprint. It's not long before I hit my stride and allow the sea breeze to blow away my worries.

Kayla

Liam is droning on about work and I'm watching Fraser run down the path to the beach, my eyes following every movement his body makes, remembering how it felt so close to mine last night.

The bed beside me had been warm when I was rudely awoken by someone knocking on the door. At first I'd thought Fraser had snuck out, perhaps regretting last night, then had changed his mind, and come back—maybe bringing something delicious for breakfast.

Then I'd almost tripped over his jeans as I'd pulled on a t-shirt and P.J. bottoms. I'd quickly searched for Peppy and saw that the pup was also missing. Fraser had been up a couple of times in the night to let Peppy out. Maybe he took the dog outside and accidentally locked the back door.

Still half-asleep, I'd unlocked the deck door before sliding it open, only to find Liam standing there. I was confused. Liam was there and Fraser was nowhere to be seen. I'd checked behind me, looking for Fraser, hoping Liam hadn't scared him off. Then I guessed he might feel uncomfortable waltzing back in dressed—or undressed—the way he was.

My confusion had been my undoing. Liam had taken over like he always does, demanding to be let in. I wasn't ready, and I hadn't taken my breaths. There was no opportunity for me to decide what I wanted. Although, to be fair, it's always more difficult to do in person.

Now he's here, relaxed and in command again. I have to find a way to break this pattern, to take control back. Closing my eyes, I thank whoever was watching over me that Fraser wasn't here to see Liam walk over me like this.

"Kayla, are you listening to me?"

"What? No, not really Liam." His face clouds over, and this time I take a breath and choose my words carefully. "I'm done, Liam. If you have problems, talk with Zuzu and Aaron."

"They aren't you, and they don't have your touch with the clients. We really need you to land these projects or I might have to lay people off."

He's so manipulative. I can't believe I never saw this when we were a couple. I roll some snappy responses round in my mind before deciding it isn't worth the effort, Liam would likely ignore me anyway.

Instead, I watch Fraser disappear from view. It is supposed to be him, not Liam, sitting here with me this morning. We should be drinking coffee and planning a day together after an amazing night. It wasn't only the physical stuff, but the talking in between, that had allowed me to believe maybe I'm ready to let Fraser in a little.

Then Liam turned up out of nowhere and undid all of that. He has spent the last half an hour talking about work, not even asking how I am. It is like we've never been apart, and I'm trying desperately to find the strength to stand up to him and ask him to leave. I don't like who I am when I'm with him. It's like I'm somehow less.

On the table in front of me are the books Fraser brought over last night, and the notebook containing my outline, a reminder of who I'd rather be breakfasting with, and who I'd rather be.

I'm rudely brought back to the here in now by Liam clasping my hand. When had he moved beside me?

"Work was just an excuse to come here. Kayla, I miss you. I miss us."

I withdraw my hand from his, unable to stop the frown from pulling my brows down. This time I draw in a breath and count to ten. Careful not to trigger his anger, I say, "Liam, it's been over for months. And have you forgotten it was you who called it off?"

He leans forward in the chair, and he's all earnest intensity that is almost creepy.

"I know, but that was when we were working together. If you're really not coming back, then we could...,"

As I listen to him, I can't breathe. It's like Liam is pulling me under water and I'm drowning. There's no time to find the right words. I have to kick out and break for the surface before I'm lost.

"No, Liam, we can't. You hurt me, and it was rocky for a bit. But I'm over you now, and we can't go back."

For a second displeasure twists Liam's face, then it's gone, and he's all cajoling smiles. "It would be different this time," Liam says, reaching for my hand again.

Pulling away, I stand and gather the coffee mugs, giving myself time to find my centre. I need space to figure out how to brush Liam off without triggering the anger that always bubbles just below the surface, and also without burning any bridges, in case I need his recommendation for a job.

"Kayla?"

Fortunately, Barb appears down the path, saving me from having to respond.

"I see you found Kayla okay. How's the make-up going? Shall I expect one more at the get together tonight?" she asks.

She obviously doesn't see the death stare I send her, as Liam is taking centre stage, flashing her one of his charming smiles. "Sorry, probably not. I'm trying to convince Kayla to come up to Sydney for a Christmas Eve party tomorrow."

I bite back a growl, angry at Liam answering for both of us, and annoyed he thinks I'd be up for his plan after our conversation this morning. It's like my opinions don't matter and I won't fall back into that abyss. "Liam, I'm not—"

"Oh, it would be a shame not to come to the Christmas drinks now you're here. You and Kayla could still head back to Sydney tomorrow and be there in time for the party." Barb carries on chatting, although she's too astute not to have noticed the tension. Fraser told me last night how protective she is of him. Is this her way of keeping us apart? Or does she really think she's helping the course of true love by throwing Liam and me together?

Liam cocks his head to the side. I can't believe he's actually considering this, and I need to put a stop to whatever he's thinking.

"Liam, I don't want—"

He talks right over me. "You know, Barb, I *could* stay the night. I have an overnight bag in the car."

"Excellent. I'm always happy to help the course of true love."

Wait, what the? Liam must have told her he was here to

make things up with me, and she really thinks this is helping me out.

"Kayla, there are clean sheets in the linen press."

Liam winks outrageously, and says, "Oh, we won't be needing those."

I clench the tray until my knuckles turn white. It takes all my energy not to clock Liam round the head with it. Unfortunately, experience tells me that contradicting Liam in front of someone when he is like this is likely to result in him verbally attacking me, reducing me to shreds. I need to keep my sense of self worth if I'm to have any chance of getting rid of Liam once and for all, so I have to avoid that at all costs. That means playing along, at least for the moment.

"I'm going to dress," I say through gritted teeth.

"Okay. Why don't I take you out for brunch? Put on something pretty."

I storm into the cottage. Not that Liam will notice. He's so caught up in his fantasy of us he can't see reality. What I need is to get him away from here. Take him somewhere public where I can lay down the law, and he won't act out.

Then, hopefully, by the time we get back here, he'll have decided to return to Sydney, and I can get on with my holiday. I try not to think of the other options; the ones where he will ignore what I say, or worse still, wait until we are alone to point out all my failings and why I'm so lucky I have him to help me be a better person.

As I shower, I remind myself this is all in my control. I do not have to be with Liam, and I am a better person without him. After last night with Fraser, I have an added incentive to remove Liam from my life. I know I can't begin something new with someone else until I can prove to myself I'm strong enough to say no to Liam. Only then can I dispel the fear that what happened with Liam will happen again.

I dress in some linen trousers and a t-shirt. Definitely not "pretty". As I fold Fraser's clothes, I allow myself a moment to breathe in the scent of him, and a wave of longing almost floors me.

"I'm sorry, Fraser," I whisper into his t-shirt, "I hope this hasn't mucked things up between us, but I need to do this alone if I'm to enjoy any time I have with you."

Placing his clothes on top of the dresser, I glance over at my mobile phone. If only I had his number, I could text him and apologise, and ask him to give me a day to sort Liam. But we hadn't exchanged numbers because of my stupid off-the-grid thing. Frustrated at not being able to at least give him a heads up, and aware Liam being here may have ruined everything with Fraser, I take my feelings out on the bed linen as I strip my bed and throw the sheets into the washing machine. I make up my bed, then take additional delight in doing the same to the bed in the spare room.

"This is where you'll be sleeping, Liam, whether you like it or not." I give the pillow one last thump for emphasis.

By the time I'm done, I come out and find Liam going through my stuff on the table.

"I don't remember inviting you to look through my stuff," I say, my voice dripping with ice as I snatch the story boards from him.

"I was just looking. You didn't use to mind me going through your work."

"That was when you were my boss and it was work, and it was the property of the business you run. This is personal."

Tears form in my eyes as my stomach burns with anger, feeling my resolve to make sure Liam gets the message that we're over.

"But we're—"

"Ex colleagues."

"Friends," Liam counters, "who are about to become more than—"

"Friends don't go prying into their friends' things." This isn't worth it. He'll never understand. "Come on, let's go have breakfast."

Fraser is running up the path as Liam and I walk across the deck. The sight of him is the one good thing about this morning. He spots us, and the hurt in his eyes, even though it's only there for a moment, tears at my heart.

Sending all the reassurance I can in my smile, I say a bright and cheery, "Hey, Fraser. I've had an unexpected friend visit. Maybe you have time before the get together tonight for a drink and a chance to meet him."

I know it's clumsy, but I hope Fraser gets the message that I want to be with him, and that Liam is only a friend. I'm so not good at this sort of thing.

Before he can respond, Liam places a proprietary hand on my arm and guides me down the steps. A cloud passes over Fraser's face, and he's gone before I can distance myself from Liam.

Fraser

Turning away from the sight of Kayla's ex leading her off the deck, I try to squash down the hurt. Not even telling myself I've only known her a few days helps. Last night was enjoyable—more than enjoyable, if I'm honest—but it was impulsive, and it doesn't give me a right to be upset.

Although..., if I think about it, there's something off about Kayla's body language. She had a smile for me, and she invited me over for drinks. When Liam led her off she had seemed to stiffen, or am I simply seeing what I want to see?

I spend the morning pottering around cleaning up the house, keeping an ear out for their return. Then I post a few things on my socials to keep the publishers happy and respond to a few comments on posts. Time drags, and I don't know what to do with myself.

As I've left the start of my book outline at Kayla's, I print it out again to read through. Then, because I was up so early this morning, I decide to make myself a sandwich while I wait. Setting up in my office, because I don't want to be distracted by the goings on next door, I begin on detailed chapter outlines for my historic mystery, researching online as I go. I don't realise how much time has passed until my phone buzzes on the desk.

Isla pops onto my screen. "Hey bro, how's things?"

"Great," I say, dredging up some enthusiasm. "Do you want to meet Peppy?"

She grins. "Of course. I know you said you were excited about him, but you really are, aren't you?"

Although I'd sent Isla a text thanking her for Peppy, it clearly wasn't enough to convince her.

"I love him, sis, and he's already got me trained."

I swivel my chair around as Isla tells me, "Dean and I hate to think of you living in such an isolated place, writing all the time. We thought you could use some company. We talked about it and agreed this was a cool way of fixing that. And Barb helped us sort it, bless her."

"You know Barb lives here too, and there are guess around all year, and town is only a short drive away. But I'm grateful you were both so thoughtful, and he's already so much a part of my life I can't imagine him not being here."

"Yeah. You know if you train him right, you can probably even take him on local signing tours with you. You know they have pet friendly hotels now."

"Hey, let's not get carried away. Here he is." I pick up Peppy and let him nuzzle the screen.

"Oh, he's so adorable," Isla gushes.

I get serious for a moment. "Isla, I know Barb organised a deal for you, but are you sure you should—"

"Hush. I wanted to do it. Dean got a bonus, and we both wanted to thank you for helping us out and"—she grins—"I got a new job. I start when the kids go back to school."

"That's great news."

"It really is. It's better hours, so we don't have to pay childcare, which is good because I'm starting at the bottom again."

"You'll soon work your way up, and you'll be running the show in no time flat," I tell her, a little giddy with her news.

"And we should be able to start paying you back as well."

"There's no rush, Isla."

My sister wrinkles her nose in the way she does when she's about to ignore me. "There is, Fraser. We appreciate what you did for us, but I know you can go quite some time without getting paid, and I don't want you to be worrying about money."

I love my sister, and I love that she understands the situation I'm in. And, even if she doesn't know it, I love that she's just helped me get a step closer to taking some time to take a new direction with my writing.

"If you can afford it, then I can't say it won't be a help."

She grins. "Anyway, I just wanted to say hi and check you're really not coming for Christmas. There's still a bed for you here. Peppy'd be welcome too."

"Sorry, Isla, I don't want to spend the next ten hours on the road. Besides, Barb is having welcome drinks for Sam and Justine tonight, and I can't leave before then. And there's the town Christmas Eve Bonfire on the beach tomorrow night, and Barb's for Christmas Day. I'm all sorted."

"Oh, I love the bonfire. Anyone good playing?"

"Just the usual locals, and some DJ from Sydney."

"Still..," she says wistfully.

"Anyway, I won't be alone over Christmas, so quit worrying about me."

"I thought you'd say that, but I had to try one last time. Christmas isn't the same without you, and I miss you."

I swallow the lump forming in my throat. Although staying here is the sensible thing to do, the reality of not spending Christmas with Isla is more difficult to deal with than I thought. "Yeah, I miss you too, sis. But I'll be up in less than a month for the book tour."

"That seems like ages away."

She sounds so much like her teenage self; I chuckle. It seems like a long time though, and I feel her pain. "You could always bring the kids down here for a week."

"That's what Dean said. But he's working all hours at the moment, and it isn't fair to him."

"I love that you two support each other—it reminds me of Mum and Dad."

"Oh, Fraser, you'll have me bawling in a minute."

I don't want to say that I'm close to tears myself. Instead, I tell her, "Call me on Christmas Day so I can see the kids open their presents."

"Love you. Oh, and make sure you get all the goss on Harry and Gretchen from Justine, unless they're coming down to visit their parents, in which case you can get it directly from them."

I ignore that last comment. She knows I'll do that without being told. "Love you too, and give my love to everyone there."

I hang up before brushing unshed tears from my eyes and snuggling my face into Peppy. "I miss them, dude."

He wriggles a little, and I put him on the floor.

"Time for a cuppa, I think."

I laugh at myself. I'm already in the habit of talking to the dog. He follows me into the kitchen, and I give him a treat while I wait for the kettle to boil. As I pour water over the tea bag, I glimpse Kayla and the ex through the side window. She's not as on edge as earlier, but I can't tell if they're now a thing from this far away.

My phone beeps, telling me it's time to tidy up and get ready for tonight. I'm itching to carry on with my book, and I've made a tea. For a second, I consider giving myself an extra half an hour before changing and heading over to Barb's. Then I remember I said I'd help her with the barbecue, and I pour out the tea before going into the office and shutting down my laptop.

After a quick shower, I pull on a plain white t-shirt and cargo shorts. Slipping my feet into flip-flops, I'm on my way out the door when, I don't know why, but I quickly nip back into my bedroom and grab a shirt to wear over-top.

Making my way to Barb's, I stop and almost return home when I realise the shirts about not letting Kayla's visitor think I'm a slob. Grinning at my vanity, I grin. *Dude, you have it bad.*

Kayla

Dressed in clean linen trousers and a silk singlet top, I've gone for subdued but not sexy for the get-together tonight. With the overtures Liam's been making all day, I don't want to give him the impression I'm dressing for him.

While we were out, I told him on no uncertain terms that we will never get back together, that I'm happy to remain friends, but that's all. He seemed to take it on board, but when I suggested he head back to Sydney, he said that would be rude since Barb had invited him tonight and he'd accepted.

I let that go, believing I'd won, but as we wandered around town after lunch I realised five minutes after I had made my stand, he'd forgotten what I'd said. When I'd suggested he change in his room, the spare room, he had chosen the bathroom instead. I'm sure he ignored me because he's still hopeful we'll share a bed, despite my telling him straight up there will never be an us again.

Even though I want to, I don't reiterate my stance, as I don't want to deal with a cranky Liam at the party tonight. I'm not ready for the people I'm going to spend the next couple of months with to see him treat me that way, and especially not Fraser. However, I will make things clear again when we get home after.

While he finishes getting ready, I pull the gateau selection Liam insisted on buying from the ritzy cake shop in town and the bottle of over-priced bubbly from the fridge. Once I would have thought this was perfect, and it is for a get together in inner-city Sydney. Out here the crowd is far more relaxed and I worry it's a little ostentatious.

Liam emerges dressed in smart trousers, a designer shirt, and loafers, looking like he's going sailing on Sydney Harbour. He raises an eyebrow when he sees me.

"Aren't you dressing up?"

"I've already told you we're at the beach, Liam. It's way more casual here."

He laughs as if I'm making a joke, but he doesn't get it. I'm pretty sure he's never had a beach holiday like this in his life. I shove the cakes at him—he can carry his own offering —and walk past him to open the door.

Glancing back over my shoulder, my drawings are calling to me. I reluctantly close and lock the door, leaving my book behind. I've lost a day working on it, a day where I could have generated new ideas and talked them over with Fraser tonight. Liam has to go tomorrow, even if I have to enlist some help to shift him.

We're the last to arrive. Over by the barbecue, Fraser is deep in conversation with the newcomers. Of course, he mentioned he's known them for years. I try to catch his eye so I can send him some sort of apology for Liam being here, but Barb turns up to take our food and drink before he sees me.

Our hostess provides us with Pimm's cocktails, and it's all I can do to sip mine daintily. A little alcohol boost might make this night a little easier, but I want a clear head for later when I confront Liam.

I'm about to join Alice and Charles for a little moral support when the Frawley kids dive under the table and start cooing. There's a little yip. Ah, Peppy, the kid magnet is under there.

"Isn't someone responsible for those unruly children?" Liam asks.

"They're just being kids," Fraser says as he ducks down and ushers them out one by one. "Let Peppy sleep, guys. He's only a baby, and this is too much excitement for him."

Peppy follows them out as far as his lead will go, tail wagging, wanting to play. Before I can introduce Liam, the new guy calls Fraser to come help with the steaks.

"You go, I'll make sure he's okay," I tell Fraser as I unclip Peppy's lead and pick him up.

The puppy nestles into my arms as we join Alice and Charles. Now and then, Liam glares at Fraser. I tap him on the arm. "Stop it."

"Who is that?" he hisses close to my ear.

"Oh, Fraser MacIntosh. He has the place next to mine."

"Fraser MacIntosh, like the author?"

I'm surprised Liam has even heard of him because I don't recall ever seeing him with a book.

"Yep, just like the author."

As we sit down, Liam manoeuvres me so I'm sitting between him and the seat Alice had been in moments before. She returns and places her youngest in her lap.

"You can sit here beside Peppy, but you let him sleep," Alice says.

I introduce Liam to everyone as my friend from Sydney, and as Charles asks how the writing's going, Liam stands abruptly and takes my glass. "I'll freshen these up," he says.

"Interesting guy," Alice says, sending me a big wink.

"I don't think family parties on the beach are his thing."

Charles barks out a laugh. "Well, clearly not. Barb's cornered him, so while he's away, you can fill us in. Is it true he's your boyfriend, and that he turned up here without being invited?"

Alice rubs Charles's arm affectionally. "You have no subtlety."

"No, it's worse than that. He's my ex," I explain, glancing up from under my lashes, hoping Fraser is listening in, but he's concentrating on the barbecue.

"Oh," Alice's eyes widen. "Soon to be not ex?"

I shake my head. "No, he'll always be an ex."

"Steaks are done," Fraser says.

Although I'm relieved the call to food has let me off the hook, part of me wishes Fraser had been close enough to listen in. I'm worried his distance tonight means I've blown things with him.

Peppy is snoring softly in my lap, so I get up and place him gently back in his crate, clipping his lead back on, before joining the adults around the big indoor table Barb has set with all the Christmas trimmings. She has the kids sitting outside with plates on their laps, and they seem happy not to have to sit and behave properly at the dinner table.

The wine and conversation flows, and for a while I forget I'm annoyed at Liam, and that I want to talk to Fraser about last night. I just enjoy the moment. Around 10 o'clock, Alice leaves to put the children to bed and Liam makes noises about our going too.

"You can leave if you want. The spare bed's made up and ready for you. In fact, if you're driving back to Sydney tomorrow, perhaps you should get an early night."

A brief flash of annoyance crosses his face. "No, it's okay. I'll stay if you want to."

"You're heading back to Sydney tomorrow?" Alice asks as she rejoins us.

I take a mug of decaf coffee from Barb and almost drop it as Liam says, "*We're* heading back tomorrow for Christmas."

Fraser gets up to check on Peppy as I glare at Liam. I haven't agreed to any such thing, and I don't want Fraser to think that I have.

"Liam, I'm not—"

"Peppy's not there." Fraser looks at me, the pup's lead dangling from his hand.

"I made sure I clipped it back on him," I say defensively, but I doubt myself under his scrutiny.

"I saw her do it," Alice comes to my rescue.

"Then where is he?" Fraser asks.

As the rest of us search the deck and immediate area, Alice slips away. A few minutes later, she returns, the pup squirming in her arms.

"Ellie snuck back and took Peppy to bed with her," Alice tells us.

Fraser takes the dog, relief he is safe written on his face. He tucks Peppy under his arm. "This is what you get for charming children," he says as he scratches behind the dog's ear.

We're all filing back inside when car headlights sweep the deck.

"Anyone expecting guests?" Barb asks.

We all shake our heads.

"It's probably just someone needing directions then," Barb says as she makes her way up to the carpark.

Minutes later, the car pulls out of the driveway, and Barb reappears..., followed by my mother, who is trundling two large suitcases.

"I've left your father," she announces as she reaches me.

Fraser

Barb pulls together a plate of food for our visitor, while Kayla talks quietly with her mother. Kayla then leads her mother up the path to her cottage, and Barb hands the plate to Liam, shooing him after them. All this time, no one speaks. I can't help feeling that this is the perfect ending to a bizarre evening. Kayla is clearly back with her ex. Peppy went missing, and now Kayla's mother has turned up saying she's left her father.

Peppy's warm body snuggles into my arms, and I pull him close, grateful for his presence. I don't think I could have stood losing him and Kayla in the same day. Telling myself Kayla wasn't exactly mine to lose, only makes me draw him closer.

I take a drink of coffee and reach for a ginger biscuit.

"That Liam's an interesting chap," Sam says.

"That's one way of putting it," I respond.

It's really bugged me how Liam had been marking his territory all night. Making sure Kayla was by his side. Talking about things they had done or would be doing. The snipes at me, clearly a threat as the only other single male in the room, becoming increasingly cutting.

I kept waiting for Kayla to tell him to pull his head in, but she alternated between ignoring him, or sending him dagger glares, or allowing him to over-talk her when she went to object to something. This Kayla is not the strong, independent woman I've been getting to know, and it makes me wonder how she can be with a guy who treats her that way.

"Sorry about Ellie," Alice says as she catches me hugging Peppy again. "I'll bring her over to apologise tomorrow."

"It's okay," I tell her, feeling magnanimous now Peppy is safe and sound. "Kids will be kids."

"She's obsessed with dogs," Charles says. "Funny thing is, she only had to wait until tomorrow. We're picking up a puppy for them as a Christmas present. I've a good mind to call up and—"

"Charles Frawley, you will do no such thing! It will do the kids good to have a dog of their own to care for, and to understand how gut wrenching it is to have one disappear on you."

"I'll still be the one who ends up walking it," Charles mock groans, and we all laugh.

Barb brings out the good brandy she saves for Christmas and pours us all a snifter. "I think tonight calls for a little nightcap before bed."

As the others sip away, Barb leans in and says so only I can hear, "Well, I got that guy wrong."

"Sorry, what?"

"When I met Liam he seemed such a lovely guy, telling me how he'd come down to win Kayla back. Now I'm thinking the Kayla wasn't too happy about him being here wasn't because she was playing hard to get, but because she didn't want him here. I can't understand what she see's in the guy."

"Ditto," I say.

"I can see you wanting to rescue her. Had things between you gone further than I thought?"

I sigh. "Yes. I don't know. I was hoping.... Are you going to tell me 'I told you so'?"

She snorts a laugh. "I wouldn't waste my breath. I will give you a piece of advice though, hard earned from being married to a jerk for several years. If you want to pursue something with Kayla, then you need to give her some space. She's got a bit to deal with at the moment with her mum, but, more importantly, she needs to finish things properly with Liam."

"So keep away all together?" I'm not sure I can do that. All I want to do is go over and wrap my arms around Kayla and to help her make everything all right.

Barb shrugs. "You can be there if she asks for help, but in the long run, it will be better for her if she breaks away from Liam herself. A relationship like that can take a toll on your mental health, and it's easier to heal if you were the one who walked away."

Barb had talked about her marriage in the past, but tonight I get the impression she has only told me a little of what she went through. Putting aside my angst, I try to lighten the atmosphere.

"Interesting advice, if a little confusing," I tease. "Back off, but be there to help?"

She mock swipes at my head before moving her attention back to the general conversation. I get what she's saying, though. Maybe things aren't okay with Kayla and Liam, but that's something for Kayla to sort out. All I can do is let her know I'm here if she wants support.

We spend the next half an hour organising who's bringing what to the Christmas Eve bonfire tomorrow night, and a short time later Alice and Charles leave. Sam and Justine stay to help clear up. Not really wanting to be at home with my own thoughts, I offer my services, but I'm sent home once we've cleared the table, as there isn't enough room for the four of us in the kitchen.

As I approach Kayla's place, I hear two female voices on the deck. Sticking to the shadows, I creep past, not wanting to disturb anyone. I do, however, glimpse Liam watching something on TV while Kayla sits with her mother on the deck.

"He only bought me the cruise because he felt guilty after the affair," her mother is saying.

"Mum, Dad's been too busy to have an affair. And Jenna has had the same boyfriend since she and Declan were at school together. Aren't you guys invited to their wedding in April?"

I hurry past. This is private stuff, and I feel cheap listening in. I put Peppy to bed, but I'm too wired to sleep and too tired to write. I make myself a hot chocolate and pick up a book before curling up under a blanket on the deck.

The murmur of female voices from next door reminds me Kayla is close by. It wasn't until her ex showed up that I realised how much I've come to care for her. Although I'd berated myself for a twice cursed fool when Liam showed up with Kayla tonight, Barb's words have given me renewed hope that we could be more than a one-night stand. The Kayla I know is worth waiting for and, although I'll hold a little of my heart back for the moment, I will give her time to decide what she wants.

Feeling a little more settled, I sip my drink and lose myself in the story.

Kayla

"She's cunning that Jenna. She's got everyone believing she's in love with that boy, but she's been seeing your father on the side."

They probably hear my eyes roll down in Sydney. This is so unlike Mum. I can't understand what exactly has set her off.

"Mum, why don't you calm down and tell me what happened on the cruise to make you leave the ship?"

"How about you make us some tea and I'll tell you," Mum counters.

Counting to ten, I attempt to control my irritation. Then I think maybe tea's a good idea after all. I can also check with Declan while I make it.

As the door slides back, I hear a noise from the bedrooms. Liam. I'd forgotten he was here. I open the hallway door and check the guest room. It's empty. I find Liam undressing in my bedroom.

"What the hell, Liam."

"I was tired, and I thought...," He gestures to the bed.

"Well, you thought wrong."

As if I don't have enough going on with Mum. I storm

into the bathroom and open the linen press, pull out blankets and a pillow and hand them to Liam.

"I have a family emergency, so I'm sure you can work out the sofa bed in the living area."

"But, after today…, I thought we were getting on so well."

I shake my head. He only thought that because he ignores everything I say. He'd clearly "forgotten" our conversation over brunch about never going out with him again—ever. How am I going to make him understand when he doesn't respect me enough to consider my feelings?

Turning on my heel, I make my way to the kitchen and busy myself making tea, and plucking up the courage for the scene Liam's about to make. When he appears, I finish up before confronting him.

"Liam, I need you to listen to me. It *is* over between us. In fact, it's been over for months. I don't know how many ways I can say it before you believe me. If it wasn't so late, and we weren't so far from Sydney, I'd prove it by kicking you out now. But I want you gone first thing in the morning."

I'm aware of Liam's eyes narrowing as he readies himself for the attack I've feared all day. Instead of flinching, I square my shoulders. I'm tired of tip-toeing around him and bending over backwards to avoid a confrontation. I can't live my life this way. Besides, I have more important things to worry about.

"Liam, right now I need you to behave like a grownup and accept this as a done deal, because I don't have the energy to play games with you anymore."

Before he can say anything, I take Mum's and my tea onto the deck, leaving Liam to sort himself out. As I sit, I feel a moment of euphoria. It's as though there was a band around my heart constricting it, and I've just broken free of it.

I look longingly over at Fraser's place. I thought I'd seen him walk by a few minutes ago, and I wanted nothing more than to call out, to call him over and to tell him that maybe, just maybe I am up for a holiday fling, or at least exploring future possibilities with him. Unfortunately, I have other priorities tonight, and I turn my attention back to Mum.

As she sips her tea, I turn on my mobile and wait for it to connect to data. It takes a couple of seconds, then it pings as message after message from Declan comes through.

"If they're from your father, you can ignore them," Mum tells me.

I carry on scrolling down through the messages to the last one.

Mum's now missing. Call when you get this, whatever time.

I head down off the deck towards the beach. When I'm far enough away that Mum can't hear me, I call Declan. He answers immediately.

"Sis, Mum's—"

"Here. She turned up spouting off about Dad having an affair, and you'll never guess who with?"

"Jenna, who I used to go to school with."

"He isn't, is he?"

"Don't be daft. She's been with Iain since senior school. They were on the cruise with Mum and Dad, and two other couples from work."

"What? For real?"

"Yep, the big job Dad did this year was for a director of the cruise line. As a thank you, he discounted a cruise for everyone who worked for him. Dad bought a deluxe one month cruise, but the others are only on for the Christmas leg to Fiji."

"Didn't Dad tell Mum this?"

"Of course he did, but she wouldn't listen. She disembarked in Auckland yesterday and didn't tell him."

"Wow, that's so not like Mum," I say, glancing up to check she's not listening in.

"Dad's flying into Brisbane tomorrow morning. When I tell him where Mum is, no doubt he'll want to pick up a rental car and come and get her and take her home."

"I don't think that'll work," I say. "She doesn't want to speak to him."

"Mmm, any ideas then?"

I pace backwards and forwards for a bit.

"How about you drive down with Dad, I drive up with Mum, and we meet half-way? It'll be neutral ground, and you and I can act as mediators."

"Do you think you can get Mum to do that?"

"I can only try. Let's leave that as the plan unless I text otherwise."

I return to the deck.

"Was that your dad?"

"No, it was Declan. He's worried about you. He said there were others from work on the cruise too, not just Jenna."

"Yeeesss."

"Mum, is it possible you got it wrong, and that Dad isn't having an affair?"

"He was with them all that first night, Kayla. Celebrating

the win, he said. And he was telling me how wonderful Jenna is and what a bright future she has, and I felt so..., old..., and useless. When I said to him I thought this cruise was for us, he said it will be later on. I was so angry I accused him of having an affair. I guess if you repeat something often enough, you begin to believe it."

"Mum, how long have you been feeling this way?"

She wraps her hands around the mug, as if she's drawing comfort from the warmth. "You young ones, you all have your careers and your own lives. I was just a mum. And now I'm not a mum any more."

"You'll always be my mum," I say automatically, but the words don't soothe mum, they anger her.

"And I guess that's all I'm good for. I should just settle back at home and knit my life away."

"Hell, Mum, you're only fifty-nine. There's still a lot of life left in you yet."

She places her cup on the table. "I don't feel like it sometimes."

"Well, you're not sitting round here moping your life away. I won't let you."

"Sometimes you sound so like your father." She doesn't sound accusatory, more defeated.

"Speaking of Dad, do you still love him?"

Mum looks pained as I ask the question. "I guess so, otherwise why would it hurt so much when he spends so much time talking to other women?"

I can think of plenty of reasons, but perhaps Mum's not ready to hear them yet.

"Okay, next question. Do you want to sort things out with him?"

This time, Mum takes a little longer to answer. "I guess I want to talk with him—really talk. Not a passing conversation, but a talk about us, and where our life goes from here."

I want to ask why they haven't had that conversation already. It's been years since Declan and I have lived at home. And Dad must be nearing retirement age. Surely they've spoken about retirement, or not retiring, or whatever it is they want to do.

"Don't look at me like that, Kayla. Everyone's relationship is unique."

"But you get you need to talk to Dad and tell him how you're feeling."

"Yes, I know. I've put it off long enough."

"And you need to find something to do that makes you value yourself."

She glances up, her eyes dagger sharp. Before she tells me off, I say, "It's only what you'd tell me."

Her eyes soften, and she laughs. "True, but it's never great to hear your own words come back out of your child's mouth. Besides, perhaps you need to take a little of your own advice."

"I don't know what you mean."

Mum leans in towards me, eyebrows raised. "Young Liam in there. He never saw you for who you were, and I never liked the way he treated you. You finally got rid of him. Now he's back?"

"He understands he's only a friend, although it's taken a bit of convincing." I can't lie to my mum.

"Good, because you need to be with someone who values you how you are, not who wants you to fit into their life."

"Yes, Mum," I say, and my thoughts go to Fraser. To how he's helped me with my novel, and how he opened up to me about his own writing. Getting to know him has been exciting, and I've slowly been able to open up to him, to trust him. I hope I haven't ruined what's happening between us.

"But, back to you. Declan said he would bring Dad down this way tomorrow, and we'd drive up and meet them so you can chat somewhere neutral."

Mum shrugs. "I'm okay to meet with him, and I guess nothing else will distract him this way…, but I'm not promising anything."

Finally, I relax back into my chair and finish my now lukewarm tea. I'm exhausted, and Mum's also looking a little worse for wear. Picking up my phone, I let Declan know we'll be heading north early tomorrow morning.

"I'm ready for bed," Mum says.

So am I—more than ready. We sneak through the living room, and I make sure Mum's got everything she needs before heading to my bedroom. I'm sitting up in bed, book in hand, when I hear something in the hallway. I move to get out of bed and find Liam standing in the doorway, dressed only in P.J. bottoms, looking damn fine, reminding me he had had some attractions. Shaking the thought off, I slump back against the pillows. I'm too tired to go through this again.

"Liam—"

"Look, Kayla, I know I came at this all wrong. I arrived here expecting to find you still broken-hearted, and that we'd pick up where we left off. I think I mis-read the whole situation."

Damn straight.

"Liam, you didn't break my heart. It was more of a hurt pride sort of thing."

"Ouch."

"What's more, when you split up with me, it made me re-evaluate what I want from life, and we just don't have a future together. I hope we can be—"

"Friends?" He smiles wryly as he sits on the edge of my bed. I tense, but he's not looking at me. "Funny thing, I've known you for five years and I didn't know you painted. Your artwork is fantastic. You should do something with it."

I know he wants me to smile, but I'm still not sure this isn't some sort of ploy. "I would love to, but it doesn't pay much."

He shrugs. "Probably not, but I sometimes wonder if focusing on earning money's all it's cracked up to be. I bet your neighbour next door is happier doing what he does than I'll ever be working in IT." He laughs self depreciatingly, showing me a side Liam I haven't seen since before we went out.

"You may be right," I say, but I think to myself, *money certainly helps.* And Liam isn't one to talk. He's always had money, so he has no idea how difficult life is without it.

"You know, I was a better person when I was with you, Kayla—I liked who I was when we were together."

I shake my head, not believing what I'm hearing, and I know if I don't say this now, I will regret it forever. "I'm sorry, Liam, but I never felt the same. When I was with you, I never felt seen. I never felt like I mattered as a person."

Liam's eyes widen with surprise. "But everyone said we were a great couple, and we were always so in tune."

"Liam, I don't say this to hurt you, but you need to hear it. We only worked well together because any time I disagreed with you, you steam rolled over me. Or you got so angry it became easier to just go along with you."

There, I've said it. I don't know if Liam will take it on board, but I feel lighter.

"I only did it—"

"God help me, Liam, if you say you only did it because you know what's best for me, I think I'll scream."

If I had punched him in the face, I don't think Liam would have been any more shocked.

"You really feel that way about us?"

I nod.

Liam runs a hand through his hair, blinks his eyes a few times, then stands. "I guess there really isn't any more to say, is there?"

I tense for the explosion, for the attack that somehow turns everything around and makes it all my fault. But Liam just stands there looking completely lost, as if someone flipped his entire world upside down.

"I heard you're getting up early to take your mother north. Don't worry, I'll be gone before you and I won't bother you again."

I have to admit, there is a part of me that feels sorry for Liam, but a bigger part of me feels pride. It was one thing for me to realise Liam's hold over me after he dumped me. It's way more liberating to break free from that hold myself. But I *am* free now, and I know I will never let anyone take over my life like that again.

As I snuggle under the covers, my thoughts turn to Fraser and I reach out and touch the place where he slept last night —I wish he was here. Now I've banished the ghost of Liam, I'm ready to allow that he is a different type of guy all together. He hasn't tried to force his plans on me, but instead has been a guiding force in helping me chart my own path.

I want nothing more than to rush over and tell him I'm ready for something more than friendship, but it's way after midnight, and I have people here. If everything goes to plan, I'll be back here tomorrow evening, and I can explain every-thing and tell him how I feel. I just hope it won't be too little, too late.

CHAPTER 7
FINALLY, BEACH MUSIC

Fraser

I check Peppy is safely in his crate, and Juno, the Frawley's kelpie, is in hers before sitting on the rug nearby. A very sorry Ellie has offered to look after them tonight, to make up for taking Peppy yesterday.

On the other side of the bonfire, people are dancing. Ellie looks longingly over at her brother and sister, but doesn't ask to leave. I don't mind keeping her company when the others get up. It's been a good day work wise, but I simply can't shake the melancholy hanging over me since I noticed both Liam and Kayla's cars had gone this morning. I'm trying hard to hold on to the hope my conversation with Barb gave me last night, but I'm scared those hopes might be dashed.

Not even an email from my agent saying the publishers had agreed to my contract changes could bring a smile to my lips. Nor could a few hours of working on my new book. By the time Sam arrived to collect me to build the bonfire and help set up chairs and tables on the beach, I needed the company to take my mind off Kayla.

It's stupid, really, I've told myself more than once. *I haven't even known her for a week and yet she's almost all I can think about.*

"Penny for them?" Barb asks.

"You'd be hard pressed to find a penny nowadays," I tell her.

She grins at me. "I don't really need to pay. That girl's clearly gotten under your skin."

"I thought we had a connection," I say rather sadly.

"Men, you can't see past the end of your noses sometimes," Barb admonishes.

"What do you mean by that?" I'm unable to keep the grumpy from my voice.

"If you did have a connection, then you should trust your feelings. If you didn't, then why are you worrying? Besides, I told you last night, give her some time."

My friend's words work their way through my fug. Does she really think Kayla might not have gone back to Sydney? Do I really think there's a chance she isn't with Liam? *This is ridiculous. I will not spend this Christmas wondering where Kayla is, and harping on what might have been.*

A local country duo takes the stage, and the music switches from canned to live. I stand and hold out my hand. "Would you like to dance, Ellie?"

The young girl giggles and stands up. "We have to stay here though, because I can't leave the dogs..., I promised."

"Right you are," I say, twirling her around in the sand by the blankets.

As the sun sets, the others in our group wander back to the picnic blankets we've set up. Baskets are unpacked, and we have quite a spread set out when I spy a figure trudging through the sand carrying a supermarket bag.

At the sight of Kayla, my heart races in my chest. Having ensured Liam isn't lurking anywhere, I allow a sliver of hope to brighten my smile as she approaches. By the time Kayla reaches us, she looks ready to drop. She holds up the bag and says, "Sorry, with driving my mum north, I didn't have time to cook."

"Don't worry about that, love," Barb says, making room for Kayla to sit. "Is your mum okay?"

Kayla shrugs. "Who knows? She and Dad are talking, and that's something."

I cock an eyebrow, wondering just what went on last night.

"It's a long story, one for another time. But she'll be fine."

"And Liam's not here?" Barb asks, a wicked gleam in her eye.

Kayla laughs. "Are you kidding? You know, I could have cheerfully killed you when you invited him to stay yesterday."

Barb winks. "But it turned out okay in the end?"

"It certainly did. He finally got my message, and last night was just about the extent of his beach holiday limits. He's probably at some swanky party tonight, and will spend Christmas with a hundred or so of his closest family and friends tomorrow."

"And you really didn't want to join him?" Alice teases.

"No, we were over ages ago. It just took him a while to accept that he's not who I want to spend my time with."

Kayla looks up from under lowered lashes, almost as if she's making sure I catch this. I hold her gaze for a beat longer until a shy smile forms on her lips, sending my senses reeling—if only we were alone. Suppressing a groan of frustration, I try to finish my food, but all I can think about is the woman sitting across from me.

We're almost done eating when Ellie leads the dogs over. The kids are gathering on the other side of the bonfire and someone's lighting sparklers for them.

"Mum?" she asks.

"Go on," Alice tells her, taking the two leads.

Peppy spies Kayla. He jumps into her lap and curls up, making himself at home.

"Did you miss me, boy?" she asks, scratching behind his ears.

I want to answer yes for both of us, but Barb distracts me by asking me to bag up the litter ready to take with us when we leave. By the time I return, Barb has moved, creating a space for me beside Kayla. "Thank you," I mouth to my friend as I settle down next to Kayla and pat Peppy.

"About yesterday," Kayla starts, her voice low so only I can hear.

"No need to explain." I tell her. "We're just friends."

"Ouch," she says. "Now I know how Liam felt last night."

A tiny glimmer of hope sparks inside me. "I'm hoping he's not just friends like we're just friends," I say with mock sternness as I drop an arm over her shoulder.

To my surprise, she wriggles back a bit and leans against

me. "No. No! Well, I mean, unless you want to be friends like Liam and I are?"

I tilt her head up so I can look into her eyes and, so that she can see the desire in mine, then bend down and kiss her. And the world disappears until the scrape of Peppy's tongue on my arm distracts me.

"So just friends?" she asks, voice husky with desire.

"Friends with possibilities," I say, thinking of the dedication I added to the first chapter of my new book this afternoon.

'To Kayla, who inspired me to take chances, and begin a new chapter in my life.'

She snuggles in to my neck. "And I hope that status comes with benefits."

I pick up Peppy and pass him to Barb, then help Kayla to her feet. Hand in hand, we join the couples dancing by the sound stage. I pull her in close and, as her body sways in time with mine, I think, *It most certainly does.*

Epilogue, Kayla

As I suck in the salty air, Peppy bounds up to greet me. Behind me, the scrunching of gravel signals a car is pulling into the carpark. I grab the leash the pup is dragging behind just in time as Peppy takes off, excited to see who's arrived.

Almost before the car stops, three children and a dog launch themselves out of the back.

"Peppy," they yell.

"Can he come down to the beach with us?" Ellie asks.

"Empty the car first," Charles tells them, and they groan. Still, they hand him Juno's lead and begin hauling bags out of the boot.

"Goodness, they've all grown so much," I say to Alice as she joins me, kissing me on the cheek.

"That's kids and dogs for you," she says. "It's good to see you again. Although I was a little surprised when I rang to book the house and Barb said you were going to be here again too."

"Barb, the most efficient grapevine I've ever met," I laugh.

"I can't wait to hear what you did this year after your month off. You in the same cottage? I'll come over for a tea when we're sorted."

"Umm, I'm not exactly alone there. Fraser's sister arrived with her family yesterday, and they're in his place."

"How does he manage to write there? It's kinda small, and with your art stuff? You are still drawing, aren't you? Did you finish your novel?"

"Woah, so many questions. I'm actually working on the second book in the series." I'm unable to keep the excitement from my voice as I carry on. "Fraser talked me into pitching it to a publisher earlier in the year, and they accepted it. I just got a very rough draft in the post this week. Alice, you're going to love your character."

Charles dumps some bags on the ground and looks up.

"You didn't say you found a place for Fraser to write in the small cottage. I can't have any delays on my next Harry Carpenter, you know."

I clutch at my chest in mock horror. "Charles, I hate to break it to you, but Fraser's publishers gave him a little leeway on the dates for the next book, and he's been working on another project."

"No way. So, no new crime book for Christmas next year?"

"It'll be out soon after though. He has the first edits back, and he's set up a workspace in the spare room so he can go through them over the next couple of weeks."

A grin splits Charles's face. "Wow, you never left, did you?"

It's more of a statement than a question. Alice's eyes widen in surprise. Peppy chooses that moment to tug at his lead, almost pulling me off my feet, into the arms of a rather sweaty Fraser who's just finished his run.

"Yuck," I say in mock dismay as I wrap an arm around his waist and hug him. "Go shower and change. Alice is coming over, and I suspect we have a lot to catch up on."

"We do indeed," she says as Fraser drops a kiss on my head before heading down the path to our cottage.

My eyes follow him as he leaves, and I bite back a sigh. With so many friends and family here, there will be no joining him in the shower. No curling up together after, and talking, or working, or reading the afternoon away. Still, we'll have the nights.

"Well, there's a turn up." Alice chuckles. "So, you never went back to Sydney? Did you find a job? Did you even look?"

I smile, suddenly shy. "No, I didn't. I found a home here. Along with my book advance, doing some cover art for a couple of publishing houses and selling prints at the local markets, I've been getting by."

Alice nudges my shoulder. "I called it. I knew you guys were always meant to be more than just a festive fling."

THE END

PART TWO

BONUS STORY, CHRISTMAS KISS

THE PUB

The air from the cooler wafts over my face, a welcome relief from the alcohol laden fug in the bar. It is busy tonight. Busier than a regular Friday.

'Get used to it,' Stan, the bar owner, says. 'It'll be like this until Christmas. Everyone and their dog'll be here ordering up their Christmas cheer.'

Plonking the wine into an ice filled bucket, I take it down the other end of the bar to the group of friends standing in a relatively quiet corner.

'Thanks, Chris, you're a star,' blonde haired Lucie tells me, handing over her card.

I flash her a smile and take it, tapping the charge before handing it back.

'It's busy tonight,' her boyfriend Dave attempts to strike up a conversation, I can just hear him over the noise.

Any other night I would have stopped and chatted with the group of friends I met on my first shift five months ago. They've sort of adopted me, and I've gotten to know them pretty well. Leena's red hair catches my eye and my heart flips over. I hate to miss an opportunity to talk to her.

'Yep,' I say, glancing down the bar, which is now about four deep. A couple of those squashed up front direct daggers my way. 'Gotta go,' I say, reluctantly turning back to the waiting horde.

'Come see us on your break,' Tony yells over the din. 'I'll shout you a drink. You'll need it by then.' The blue-eyed tech genius winks.

'Over here,' a voice shouts, and that's it. I'm rushed off my feet, literally.

The bar I tended in uni was nothing like this swanky, Central London watering hole full of traders and techpreneurs who think the world revolves around them. I miss the few locals who haunted the pub back home, and the slow pace that meant there was always time to sit and chew the fat with them.

I don't get my first break until after ten. Once Stan relieves me, I push my way through the bar towards Tony, hoping for a chance to talk tech, and maybe exchange a few words with the lovely Leena.

'Mate, you look exhausted. Here, have some bubbles,' Tony greets me, pushing a glass of sparkling liquid my way.

I would have preferred a beer, but with what I get paid and the cost of living in London, I can't afford to be choosy.

'Thanks,' I say, taking the glass and downing half in one go. As the bubbles evaporate on my tongue, there's a sharp tug on my taste buds, and moments later, the alcohol rushes to my head.

'So what's happening tonight?' I ask.

'Well, I got a promotion.' he points to the wine bottle. 'Hence the bubbles.'

'Congratulations, mate,' I say, clapping him on the shoulder.

He shrugs it off, almost embarrassed by the attention. 'Lucie's trying to organise us for New Year's, and Leena's bemoaning Christmas.'

At the mention of her name, Leena towards us. 'I'm not whingeing about Christmas, just work Christmas parties.'

Under her gaze, my heart pounds, and my palms sweat. My tongue swells to twice the size, and I lose the power of speech. I'm forced to watch as Tony, who's known the goddess Leena forever and is completely unaffected by her beauty, responds.

'How does it go again? Why does it have to be on a weekend? Why do we have to take partners? Why is it so formal?' He teases. 'I don't understand why you don't pass on it and spend the night with us.'

Leena punches Tony on the arm, and it's not a lite tap either. 'Yep, great idea, bozo. Not all of us are geniuses. Some of us have to schmooze the bosses to rise through the ranks.'

She runs a hand through her thick, long hair, sweeping it off her face. 'Besides, it's not my fault that all the men in my life are dating my best friends.' She flashes a grin at the girls, taking the sting from her words.

Antonio holds up his hands. 'Hey, I don't have a girlfriend and you didn't ask me.'

Leena drapes an arm over his shoulder. 'And any other night I would take you along. Unfortunately, Robert's told me about his plans for the weekend, and I won't spoil them.'

Antonio leans down and kisses the top of Leena's head. 'Yep, I'd have to do some quick talking if I ruined his surprise.'

'What about Chris?' Cecily says. 'He's not dating anyone?' She turns sparkling blue eyes on me, an eyebrow raised in query.

'Um…ah…no.' *Smooth bro, way to sweep a girl off her feet.*

I stare at the ground, trying to compose myself. I've a shift tomorrow night. That's as good an excuse as any to get out of this awkward situation. When I look up, Leena is standing in front of me, cat green eyes level with mine, her face mock beseeching.

'Would you, Chris? I promise it won't be too much of a chore. It's at a swanky place with great food and free drinks. And, who knows, you might meet someone you like.'

'Go on, Chris,' Cecily adds. 'Some of her workmates are real pillocks—it's all that startup venture capital bullshit. But there are also some cool people, and a few are techies, so you might make some contacts.' She slips her arm through Tony's and leans her head on his shoulder.

With the three of them staring at me, I want to say no, but the word is stuck in my throat.

Ever since I first met Leena all I've wanted to do is to ask her out, but I've never plucked up the courage. She is so confident, and beautiful, and… amazing—way out of my league.

Don't get me wrong, I do all right. Years of surfing have given me a decent body, which I keep toned in the local pool, and a tan that hasn't faded much yet. When I look in the mirror, I'm not horrified. I might not be Chris Hemsworth, but I'm a solid Liam.

Still, if I could pluck up the courage to ask her out, this is not what I would plan for a first date—a work Christmas party with everyone getting drunk, trying too hard to enjoy themselves, and crying in their drinks at the end of the evening.

'All right,' I say. 'I'll go. Text me the details.'

I thread my way back through the crowded bar to finish my shift, my stomach churning in a mixture of disappointment and anticipation.

PARTY NIGHT

I hunch into my borrowed coat as the damp permeates my bones in the way only London weather can. It's supposed to snow tonight. The English always hope it'll snow for Christmas. It's such a big deal they even bet on it happening.

As I turn into the East End street Leena texted me to pick her up from, I wonder how my family and friends are doing. A wave of sadness and homesickness hits me. I pull out my phone and text my brother.

Happy almost Christmas.

It's early morning in Sydney so I don't expect a response. I'll call tomorrow.

My phone buzzes.

Dude, it's 5am.

I chuckle.

> The barbie needs cleaning or there'll
> be no prawns for Chrissie lunch.

This time the response is immediate.

> Car's packed. We're heading up the
> coast in an hour. Christmas at the
> beach.

> Call you later.

I end, wishing I was there. Perhaps next year I'll be working in my dream job and I'll head home for a proper Christmas in the sun.

Ah, number 53, I've arrived. The building's one of many redeveloped warehouses lining the street. Before pressing the button, I try to shake off my melancholy.

So, I'm not at home, and this is not the first date I imagined with Leena. But, it *is* a date—anything could happen. Life is full of possibilities. A car pulls up behind me and honks as I press the buzzer.

'Chris?' A female voice asks over the intercom.

'Yep.'

'Is that the taxi too?'

I turn to find a traditional London black cab idling by the curb. Cool. I can normally only afford the underground, so this'll be something to tick off the bucket list.

'Yep.'

'I'll be down in a mo.'

Sheltering in the doorway out of the drizzle, I angle myself so I can see through the slat of safety glass. It's uncomfortable compared to waiting in the cab, but I'm rewarded by a glimpse of Leena as she steps out of the lift.

She's wearing an off the shoulder sparkling emerald cocktail dress that clings to her curves in all the right places. By the time she joins me, the dress is a slip of green hidden under a black coat she is doing up around the creamy skin of her neck.

For a moment I wonder what it would be like to move the stray strands of hair out of the way and brush my lips across the skin peeking out from her collar. The moment is gone when she scolds me with a curt, 'Chris, you should have waited in the cab.'

I chuckle as I open the car door for her, and attempt to lighten the mood. 'What, and have my mother's voice in my head all evening berating me for my lack of manners?'

Before she says anything to make things more awkward, I push the door shut and duck around the cab. I plonk into the seat on the other side, struggling to arrange my coat.

'Where to, love?' A West Indian accent drifts from the front. The cabbie's already identified who is running this show.

'The Hilton, Hyde Park, thanks,' Leena says, settling back as the cabbie closes the window and slides away from the curb.

'Thank you for doing this for me.' Leena talks to me, but her gaze is fixed on the view outside. 'I hope it wasn't too much trouble sorting a black-tie outfit on such short notice.'

I don't want to tell her that the only thing I'm wearing that I owned before this morning are my underwear and my shoes. Fortunately, Tony put me onto a great op-shop selling second-hand tuxes and dress shirts.

'They're last seasons or older, but they're cheaper than renting,' he'd told me.

They *were* cheap, and they had my size. While my suit and shirt spent some time in a two-hour dry cleaners, I nipped round to Tony's to pick up a tie and coat. I'll be eating baked beans on toast for the next month, but it'll be worth it —I hope.

'No worries, I always travel with a suit,' I joke, and she manages a weak smile.

The conversation falters. *Well, this is fun.* I mentally shake myself. If this was any other night, or any other girl, I'd be chatting away, trying to make a connection.

'So, anything I need to know before we enter the lion's den?'

She pulls her gaze away from the passing scenery. 'Sorry, Chris. I hate these things. I shouldn't have dragged you into my nightmare.'

Her fingers twist in her lap. She's as nervous as I am—perhaps for a different reason, but at least it's something we have in common. I smile, hoping to put her at ease.

'I assure you, I'm perfectly house trained, and can even hold a half decent conversation. I won't show you up.'

My attempt at a joke falls flat. A stricken look crosses her face. 'I didn't mean...'

'Leena, calm down. We're going to eat a meal and a few with your workmates, and when you've put in a solid appearance, we can leave. No one will be bored. No one will be embarrassed. And, if we're lucky, we might actually have some fun.'

Her shoulders relax and she returns my smile. 'You're awfully sure of yourself given you haven't met my workmates yet.'

Good, this is the Leena I know—sassy and confident.

'After working in a bar in London, I think I can handle anything they throw at me,' I tell her.

A frown creases her brow. 'Ah, about that...'

She doesn't need to say it. Not everyone is comfortable dating a mere bartender.

'It's ok. You can tell everyone I'm here working on a pitch to Pinewood.' I reassure her. 'I won't be offended.'

Her smile returns. 'You know, I forgot about your other job.'

I laugh. 'Hardly a job yet. My interview isn't until after Christmas.'

She takes my hand in hers and my heartbeat is thundering so loudly in my ears, I almost don't hear her words. 'Chris, don't talk like that, even if you are joking. To get ahead in life, you need to believe you will succeed.'

'We're here, love,' the cabbie calls, and our brief moment of connection is gone.

FISH OUT OF WATER

The tiramisu melts in my mouth, and I stifle a groan.

'It's good, isn't it?' Anabeth, the girl on my left leans in, her chocolate brown eyes twinkling with amusement.

'Good isn't close to describing it,' I tell her, rolling my eyes in ecstasy.

She laughs and takes another spoonful.

I turn to Leena, but she's still talking to the head of finance sitting on her other side. Anabeth's dinner companion is chatting to the waitress, or more specifically— chatting her up.

'He's a terrible flirt,' she confides.

'Don't you mind him paying so much attention to other women?'

She grins. 'Hell no. He's my brother, and I wish one of them would stick around long enough to take him off my hands.'

Her brother half-turns, throws her a dirty look, then follows the waitress out of the dining room.

Leena touches my arm and I turn to find she and the man she has spent most of the evening speaking to are standing. Her voice vibrates with excitement as she says, 'Neville and I are off to the bar to brainstorm! I have this incredible idea he wants to hear. You can join us if you want?'

Her tone suggests she'd be more than okay if I didn't go with her. My eyes drift to my half-eaten dessert, then back to her. 'Perhaps when I'm finished,' I say, but she's already following her boss out.

I polish off my tiramisu, and Leena's untouched one, and have some more coffee. Anabeth excuses herself to go find her brother and I head to the bar. A gaggle of men preening and vying for her attention surround Leena. I'm clearly not needed, so I make my way to the bar and order a whiskey.

'Gin and tonic,' a voice beside me says, and I move to allow Anabeth in beside me.

She was bright and bubbly company over dinner, and I hope maybe she'll stay for a bit and keep me company while I wait for Leena.

'Lost your brother again?'

She laughs. 'Yes, but he'll be back. It's all about the chase for him.'

In her heels, she is almost as tall as I am. I allow myself to appreciate her willowy form, showcased in a violet ankle-length lace number, as she waits for her drink. She really is very attractive. If I wasn't with Leena.... I push the thought from my mind. I *am* here with Leena, and Anabeth hasn't given me any reason to believe I'm anything more than a dinner companion.

'Leena's still talking shop, I see,' she says, turning to me.

We turn as one towards the group of senior execs. Leena appears unaware of the hold she has over them as she debates the merits of investing in additional functionality for the app. They follow her every word as if she's a messiah.

'Yep,' I say, unable to drag my gaze away.

'You've got it bad, huh?'

I force myself to turn away and pick up my drink.

'Sorry, what was that?'

She stares at me over the rim of her glass. 'You've got the Leena bug. It's okay. Most of the guys at work have it. We girls'd all hate her if she wasn't so unaware of the effect she has on them.'

Do I have the Leena bug? I'm definitely attracted to her, and I'd like the chance to find out. Yet, I'm not keen to admit this to the attractive woman by my side.

'I'm just her plus one for a night out at a swanky restaurant,' I finally tell her.

'Sure.' She quickly hides a brief flash of sympathy as she places her hand on my arm. 'If you say so.'

The sudden rush of heat from my neck to my face has me hoping I'm not actually blushing. I'm finding Anabeth's heartfelt sympathy as attractive as Leena's sexy confidence, and it's throwing me off balance. Desperately to change the subject, I ask, 'Do you work in finance too?'

She tucks a strand of purple streaked silver hair behind an ear, revealing a dragon ear clip that brings a smile to my lips. She is so not what I expected from a workmate of Leena's.

'No, nothing that exciting. I'm a coding a new module for the app.'

Anabeth's brother chooses that moment to join us.

'So the waitress blew you off,' she teases him.

He ignores her. 'Don't listen to her, Chris. She and her mates designed the app at uni, and she's the only one the investors kept on after the buy-out—she's irreplaceable.'

I assess my companion with fresh eyes. She is intent on squishing the lime in her drink with the straw. Her brother's comment has obviously made her uncomfortable, and I feel a protective urge to put her at ease.

'Really? You're a millionaire coder?' I joke.

'I wish.' She smiles shyly. 'The buyout was small, and I opted for shares in the company rather than cash. I won't see a dime beyond my salary until we make a profit.'

'Smart move,' I tell her. 'From what Leena says, it's going to be the new Twitter.'

Her cheeks redden, and she seems to find her drink fascinating. I frantically think of something else to say to make this fey girl smile, but I'm distracted by a presence at my side.

'I see you're keeping yourself entertained, Chris,' Leena purrs and my heart flips.

'Yep. Anabeth and... um Robbie here are filling me in on the background to the app.' I'm irritatingly proud that I managed to string a coherent sentence together.

'Would you like to come and meet some of the board?' she asks, linking her arm possessively through mine.

With her body this close, it's difficult to think of anything other than what it might be like to pull her into my arms and kiss those cherry red lips. Unfortunately, her allure will not overcome my aversion to the men she's with. A few months working in the pub has taught me I will never have anything in common with the likes of them.

'Thanks,' I tell her, 'I'm fine here.'

A frown creases her perfect brow, and she glances sidelong at Anabeth. 'If you're sure I can't tempt you away…' she pauses, giving me the chance to change my mind. When she realises I'm not moving, she says, 'All right then.'

I watch her body sway the sparkling green sheath as she returns to her group of admirers.

'Interesting,' Robbie says, bringing my attention back to the bar.

I take a gulp of whiskey before asking, 'What is?'

'The ice queen seems to have a soft spot for you.' He playfully punches me on the arm.

I turn slightly so I can't be tempted to look her way. 'She was just being polite. Making sure I'm okay.'

'Sure,' Robbie says and slides onto a stool.

In another room music starts up and a few people leave the bar. Anabeth and Robbie stay, and I notice Leena's group does too.

'So, Chris, what are you doing in London? Taking a year out and working as a waiter?' Anabeth is the first person tonight to ask me anything about myself.

I laugh. 'Not a waiter, I work in a bar.'

'Hopefully somewhere nice, away from all these London wankers…, oops, that was rude.' She takes a gulp of her drink in an attempt to hide her embarrassment.

I raise my eyebrows in mock surprise. 'You don't like your workmates?'

She shrugs. 'Not many of them, no.'

'Well I'm not too keen on them either. I serve them—or people like them—and we have nothing in common.'

'So why do you work there?' Robbie asks.

'One of mum's old friends owns the bar. He's let me have the room above for free. I couldn't have afforded to come over and spend time in London otherwise.'

Anabeth nods. Everyone who lives in London shares my pain. 'Are you saving to do Europe?'

I shake my head. 'That wasn't the plan.'

Suddenly I'm shy about telling her why I'm in England. Everyone else glazes over and changes the subject when I talk about movies and animation. Only Tony has taken me seriously—helping me with my portfolio, and honing my presentation.

Anabeth tilts her head to the side and studies me for a moment. Perhaps sensing my discomfort, she says, 'Sorry, I ask a lot of questions. You don't have to answer.'

'No, it's ok.' Suddenly I have the urge tell her about my job interview, and what I hope to do in the future. 'Since uni I've been working for a movie production company. I gave up my job to come over here to interview for the Pinewood special effects team. Before I met them, I wanted to make sure I could live in London—it's so different from home. I also wanted to make sure my presentation and portfolio are up to their standards.'

Anabeth's eyes light up and she leans in. 'Cool. What sort of special effects do you do?'

'Mostly digital, but I've done some stop frame animation on short films,' I tell her.

'Anything I might know?'

'Ana's a movie buff,' Robbie adds, before sliding off the stool. 'If you guys are going to film talk, I'm going to dance.' He saunters away, moving in time to the music, scanning the crowd for a potential partner.

'The short films I worked on were only released in Australia,' I tell Anabeth.

'Have you done any other movies?'

'There's an action one that finished production just before I left Australia. It should come out early next year,' I admit.

She frowns. 'I would have said I can't wait to see it, but action's not really my thing.'

I laugh. 'Mine neither, but you take the work where you can get it, and it looks good on my resume.'

Anabeth chews her bottom lip, then blurts out, 'Don't I know it. I'm kinda not enjoying working for the startup as much as I thought I would. I think I'll wait around for the next launch, and then I'm off.'

'Will you do something yourself, or join another company?'

'I'm not sure. I want to develop something that makes people's lives better. Our app was supposed to do that. Now they just want it to make more money. So... I'm thinking maybe freelance for a while.'

I slip onto the bar stool Robbie vacated and order another drink. It's so refreshing talking to someone who understands about giving up a job that isn't particularly satisfying to pursue your dreams.

'I'm hoping if I get into Pinewood I'll get a bit more variety, and a bit more control over what I get to do,' I tell her, and she nods in understanding.

The next hour flies by as we talk movies, and books, and music. I begin to relax and enjoy myself for the first time tonight.

EAVESDROPPERS NEVER HEAR GOOD

From of the corner of my eye, I catch Leena heading for the cloakrooms. Wondering if she's thinking of leaving, I excuse myself and follow her towards the back lobby. I glimpse a slip of green as the door to the ladies' room closes.

Finding I need the men's room, I duck in there, thinking I'll catch Leena on the way back. I finish up and am washing my hands when I hear disembodied female voices drift from the ladies' toilets next door.

One of them is definitely Leena. I step back. Yep, her voice is clear if I stand here. I nip into the cubical and close the door.

Do I feel guilty? Hell no. What person doesn't want to find out what's being said about them by a girl they're interested in?

'—doesn't see me as anything other than Tony's friend.'

If that's me she's talking about, then she couldn't be more wrong.

'Why don't you let him know you fancy him? Anabeth certainly is,' an unknown voice answers.

She is? A smile curves my lips as I think of Anabeth leaning towards me, eagerly arguing why I should give Doctor Who a second chance. Or how she tucks her hair behind her ear when she's making a point—like telling me books are always better than movies—the eyes of her dragon ear clip flashing in agreement.

'I'm not sure that's such a good idea.' Leena's voice interrupts my reverie. 'I'm only looking for someone for tonight, and I'm not sure he's my best bet. What he if wants more, or doesn't want me at all? He's friends with Tony, and I would have to see him again, which would be awkward.'

I'm good with a one-night stand, I mentally send to her. One night can turn into two, or maybe more. Or it can help be get you out of my system.

'You're a modern woman. You can do this.'

Yes, you can! I cheer her on.

'I don't know...'

'If you were a man, we wouldn't be having this conversation. A male would do it without all this soul searching.'

Woah, hold on there. Not all men. I'm not big on one-nighters. And *I* would use it to convince Leena we could have so much more.

Would you really, though? The devil on my other shoulder weighs in. *So far, Leena has shown no interest in you, and she just called you Tony's friend, not* my *friend. Are you really okay with only being a booty call?*

Shh, I tell it. *I'm listening.* But I'm too late. The only noise coming from next door is the echo of a door closing.

I let myself out of the cubicle and head back to the bar, hopeful tonight will end exactly as I'd hoped, with Leena and I leaving as a potential couple. Leena's dress sparkles through the glass of the door to the bar. In a couple of strides, I'm beside her.

'Are you ready to go?' I ask, hoping after the conversation I overheard she'll say yes.

She doesn't answer, but carries on searching the room. Was I wrong? Was she talking about someone else? The group she was with had found a bank of chairs, and they're waving her over. She holds up a finger, then turns to me.

'I want to leave,' she tells me. Her eye-slide towards the group suggests otherwise. 'But I'll never have another opportunity like this to put my ideas to the board members. You understand, don't you?'

She reaches up and runs her fingers along the lapel of my suit, and my eyes focus on her hand. I understand, and I would do the same if it were my career. I open my mouth to tell her that, but don't get a chance. She grabs my tie and tugs me into a darkened corner before pulling my head towards hers.

Her lips are firm on mine, they taste of whiskey and something sweet. My mouth is moving against hers and I can't think of anything else but her lips on mine and the warmth spreading from my belly. She nips at my lower lip and I snake an arm around her back, intending to pull her against me. She steps back before I can tighten my grip.

'Later,' she says, her eyes sparkling as she sashays away.

My eyes follow her, but not with longing. Leena is an accomplished, sexy woman, and her kiss promising more later was more than I could have expected from tonight. I should be elated, instead I feel...empty, and used.

I drag my gaze away, confused, to lock eyes with Anabeth across the room. The hurt I find there adds to the rush of emotion swirling in my head. She draws her bottom lip between her teeth, shakes her head, then turns on her heel, walking towards the coat check.

My body freezes in place as my head attempts to sort through my emotions. I half turn towards Leena. *Should I join her?* No, they don't want me with them, any more than I want their company. I turn towards the exit in time to see Anabeth enter the lift.

The only reason I've enjoyed this evening is leaving, and still I can't force my body to move. At the very least, I should apologise to her. But for what? *Leena* kissed *me*. And why does that matter to Anabeth? It's not like we had anything going? Or did we?

Then it hits me like a punch to the stomach and my legs move of their own accord. Weaving through the tables, I find the universe is against me, slowing me down as people move chairs or themselves into my path, forcing me to dodge obstacles as Anabeth gets further and further away.

Finally, I'm out. The coat check takes an age to find my coat. I haul it on as I rush down the stairs, hoping to beat Anabeth's lift to the lobby. I'm too late.

Zigzagging through a surprisingly busy entranceway, I push open the heavy glass doors and stand there shivering in the chilly night air as I search the street for her. There she is, a couple of blocks away, walking, head down, walking back towards Central London.

'Anabeth.' The drone of traffic muffles my voice. *Doesn't this city ever sleep?*

I glance warily up at the cloud laden sky. The incessant London drizzle has stopped, but the ground is still slippery under the soles of my leather dress shoes as I take off at a brisk walk after her.

Anabeth is fast, even in heels. I almost catch her up around Archway, but the lights change before I can get there. I call again. *Why is she ignoring me?* I fall into pace beside her as the path takes us around Green Park.

'Anabeth,' I say, tapping her on the shoulder.

She starts, half turns towards me with a can of something in her hand, then relaxes. Placing the container back in her bag, she reaches up and takes out her ear pods.

I shake my head. 'Are you mad? You shouldn't be walking alone at night round here, let alone with ear pods in.'

Her hand sweeps out, gesturing to the passing cars. 'I'm

not alone. Besides, I've done karate for years. And if that doesn't work, I always have pepper spray handy.'

'Still, a woman alone...'

'A woman should be able to walk alone wherever and whenever she wants, just as a man does. I refuse to be limited by my gender.'

She glares at me all purple under the streetlights, and fierce as. I can't help it. I smile at her, even though this is not how I thought this conversation would go. Then again, I'm not sure what I expected when I ran out after her. Now I'm standing there, all goofy and tongue-tied and unsure what to do next.

'Ah..., at least let me walk you home,' I say, feeling seventeen and taking Kylie Simons to our Year 12 Formal awkward —all arms and legs, and all commonsense deserting me.

'Why?'

The single word is like a slap to my senses. Why should she let me walk her home? Why do I want to walk her home? Why am I here? Or all of the above?

'Because it's the right thing to do,' I tell her, and it sounds weak to my own ears—more so after her speech on female independence.

She blows out a breath, and the anger drains from her body. 'Chris, go back to Leena. You clearly have something more going on there than you let on.'

Leena? In my rush to catch Anabeth, I'd forgotten about her. I should let her know where I am. Or, will she even notice I'm gone until she's ready for her booty call?

Anabeth, taking my moment of confusion as a sign we're done, turns on her heel and carries on walking. I fall into step beside her. We continue alongside Green Park for a while in silence. Anabeth doesn't put her ear buds back in, which I take as a good sign.

As we turn onto St. James Street, we still haven't spoken, and the silence is like a weight between us. I have to say something, but everything running through my head at the moment is perhaps not best discussed with the woman walking beside me—well not if I want to make a good impression that is.

There is no way I can explain that for months I have fantasised about being with Leena, about holding her in my arms and getting to know every luscious inch of her body. And less than half an hour ago, I had her right where I wanted her. Yep, that would really go down well.

I can't tell her I'd found out Leena wasn't interested in me as a person, only because of my body. Or how, initially, I'd been okay with that because surely, once she got to know me, there would be more.

Then, Anabeth left, and my world quaked. All I could think of as I walked to catch her up was, what if I never saw her again? I'd never know whether she thought the new Taika Waititi film was funny or not? And I promised to show her why Vegemite on toast is so great.

Silly things to be thinking of, and not things I can say out loud now to break this uncomfortable silence. How can I tell her I couldn't let all those little things we spoke about, of those possibilities of future conversations, disappear because of a kiss, no matter how good? Or even for a one-night stand?

So, I don't say any of that. Instead, I ask, 'Do you live close?'

A half-smile appears at the edge of her lips, showing off a dimple. 'Worried you won't be able to find your way back?' she asks.

I pull out my phone. 'Google Maps,' I say. 'Just wondering how far a crazy English woman is prepared to walk alone at night, in high heels when it's threatening to snow.'

That brings on a full-on chuckle. 'We Brits always hope it will snow around Christmas. And it always threatens, but never does.'

'So?'

'I live in a flat over a bookshop on Charing Cross Road. Not too much further.'

I raise an eyebrow. 'Man, that must cost a bit to rent.'

'Are all you Aussies so blunt?' she asks.

Her tone is humorous, so I know I haven't offended her. 'Probably,' I say.

'I work Saturdays for my uncle in the shop, and in return, he doesn't charge me too much for the flat. It suits me because it's walking distance to work, and I love books.'

'Nice,' I say.

Now the lull in the conversation feels normal. All too soon, we arrive at the National Gallery and turn the corner, entering Trafalgar Square. My breath catches, and when Anabeth stops walking, I realise I must have sighed out loud.

Trafalgar Square is pretty iconic at the best of times, and I often have to pinch myself when I walk around it to make sure I'm really here. At night time, under the glow of lights, with a dark, cloudy sky as a backdrop, it's breathtaking.

Something cold touches my nose, and I'm about to curse the London rain when the world becomes a vision of glitter and ice as snow falls. My mouth stretches into the widest grin and I allow Anabeth to haul me into the square.

I stretch my arms out and spin around like a child, giddy with the joy of it. When I stop, Anabeth is watching me, her eyes bright with laughter, enjoying my happiness.

In a split second the world fades away, and there is only Anabeth and me. I step towards her. A flash of fear crosses her face and I pause.

'Why are you here, Chris?'

'For this,' I say as I pull her closer.

My eyes lock with hers and I lower my head, brushing her lips gently with mine. When she doesn't pull away, I close my eyes and deepen the kiss. Wrapping my arms around her, I pull her closer and shudder as her fingers reach up and tangle themselves in my hair.

Her body moulds to mine as if it has always meant to be there, and intense heat melts my limbs. My last coherent thought is, 'Yes, I'm here for this.'

ACKNOWLEDGMENTS

As an indie author I am so grateful for the family, friends and professional team I rely on to turn my story ideas into something other people might want to read.

Festive Fling started as a First Kiss kind of story with the simple idea of a beach romance for a Christmas signing. Then it got away from me a bit, but Madeline Ash from Creating Ink helped me get it back in shape.

I wouldn't have been so bold with picking up Madeline's suggestion on Kayla's and Liam's relationship without my Tuesday Coastwrite group. I had worried leaning into Liam's coercive control tendencies might be too dark for a sweet romance, but they gave me the confidence to change the story line.

As a bonus to the printed novella, I've included a re-edited version of my very first sweet romance story, Christmas Kiss.

I want to thank the lovely Nicole and my friend Ros for Beta reading my First Kiss Stories. Without a doubt, these tales would not have been what they are without them.

And thank you to AmandaJane from QuillandInk for the final polish. You can find her on fiverr.com.

And, as always, love and thanks to Jim and Sam for supporting my mad, crazy writing addiction. A special shout out to my writing buddies; my dog Trouble, who is always with me, and Lola, the cat, who insists she's trying to help every time she crosses my keyboard.

ABOUT THE AUTHOR

I am a sweet romance and cosy mystery author under the pen name Lee Williamson. I also write YA/NA Fantasy as Vivienne Lee Fraser.

I live in Sydney with my husband, son, our dog Trouble and an over-active kitten called Lola. We get to travel a lot because our family lives around the world, but there's nothing like coming home and curling up with a good book.

When I am not writing I love reading, walking the dog, craft activities and good movies.

One day I am sure I will grow up, but hopefully not too soon. If I ever do, I would like to be exactly what I am now, and what I have always dreamed I would be, a writer.

You can find me at:

https://viviennelfraser.com.au/writing-as-lee-williamson

Facebook.com/LeeWilliamsonAuthor

Instagram.com/leewilliamson66

Tiktok.com/@leewilliamson66

FIRST KISS – 12 SHORT STORIES

That First Kiss is everything. It can start a romance, end a relationship, bring back memories, or even leave you cold. First Kiss short reads are 45 minute, bite sized slices of life built around that First Kiss, with a touch of sweet romance. So grab a coffee and read.

Includes:

Christmas Kiss, A New Years Kiss, Valentine's Kiss, Easter Kiss, A Kiss From The Past, Virtual Kiss, The Lost Kiss, Purrfect Kiss, The Kiss Not Taken, Beach Kiss, A Kiss In The Dark, Illicit Kiss

<h1 style="text-align:center">THE MAGGIE AND MARPLE SERIES</h1>

Prequels to the Maggie and Marple Series. Meet Clara and Maggie as the solve their first mysteries

THE LOVE LETTER MYSTERY

A Special Book. A Love Letter. A Mystery to be Solved.

Big changes are happening in Clara's life, is now really the time to be helping her friend Sassy find the owner of a mysterious love letter?

Her boyfriend Tyrone wants her to concentrate on their future, but solving the mystery is just too intriguing to ignore.

Will Clara find the owner of the letter? And will she still have a boyfriend if she does?

London's Soho in the seventies is all glitz and glamour masking a sinister underbelly.

Having grown up in small town New Zealand, Maggie Thompson leaps at chance to live and work there. When she runs into her childhood crush, Daisy, she becomes a part of the Soho scene in a way she could only have dreamed of.

Excited and exhilarated by the bohemian culture, she thinks life can't get any better, and that's when her world crashes around her. In a single night Daisy rejects her, their friend Duke goes missing, and Maggie is introduced to the darker side of Soho.

Can Maggie help Daisy track down Duke while nursing a broken heart? And can they do it before he is lost to them forever?

MURDER IN THE MANUSCRIPTS

A hidden diary. A scrap of paper. An abandoned puppy.

Could these three clues mean that Maggie's friend Lawrence didn't die from natural causes? Maggie believes so and intends to investigate—even if her broken ankle is slowing her down.

Fresh from heartbreak, Clara travels from Sydney to country New Zealand to look after her injured great-aunt, only to find Maggie set upon investigating her friends death.

As the two women dig into how Lawrence died, they uncover a not-so-wholesome side to the township of Waiawa, one which Sargent Richardson would rather they stayed away from.

With help from her Mystery Book Club, will Maggie find out the truth about Lawrence's death? And will Marple the dog find her forever home?

A hidden body. A silk ribbon. A bouquet of flowers.

When a body is found in the walled up recess of her bookshop, Maggie's dead father falls under suspicion for murder. Determined to find the truth about the unidentified victim, Maggie starts her own investigation against the wishes of the local police.

When Marple uncovers a bouquet of flowers and a ribbon in the debris of the demolished wall, Clara is happy to track down their origin to help clear her great-grandfather's name, and to distract her from worsening relations with her ex, Tyrone.

Then Marple reveals some more disturbing evidence and old wounds are reopened. Can the Mystery Book Club solve the puzzle before a long-buried feud tears the town apart?